SAVING ARIEL

The One I Want

ELLIE MASTERS

JEM Publishing

The One I want

a series of love stories

Editor: Erin Toland

Proofreader: Rox LeBlanc

Interior Design/Formatting: Ellie Masters

Published in the United States of America

JEM Publishing

ISBN: 978-1-952625-36-7:

Dedication

This book is dedicated to my one and only—my amazing and wonderful husband.

Thank you, my dearest love, my heart and soul, for putting up with me, for believing in me, and for loving me.

You pushed me when I needed to be pushed. You supported me when I felt discouraged. You believed in me when I didn't believe in myself.

If it weren't for you, this book never would have come to life.

Books by Ellie Masters

The LIGHTER SIDE

Ellie Masters is the lighter side of the Jet & Ellie Masters writing duo! You will find Contemporary Romance, Military Romance, Romantic Suspense, Billionaire Romance, and Rock Star Romance in Ellie's Works.

Sign up to Ellie's Newsletter and get a free gift. https://elliemasters.com/RescuingMelissa

YOU CAN FIND ELLIE'S BOOKS HERE:

ELLIEMASTERS.COM/BOOKS

Military Romance

Guardian Hostage Rescue

Rescuing Melissa

(Get a FREE copy when you join Ellie's Newsletter)

Rescuing Zoe

Rescuing Moira

Rescuing Eve

Rescuing Lily

Firestorm

Billionaire Romance

Billionaire Boys Club

Hawke

Richard

Brody

Contemporary Romance

Cocky Captain

Romantic Suspense

EACH BOOK IS A STANDALONE NOVEL.

The Starling

~AND~

Science Fiction

Ellie Masters writing as L.A. Warren

Vendel Rising: a Science Fiction Serialized Novel

Chapter One

Ariel

HURRICANE JULIAN IS THE TENTH STORM OF THE SEASON. THE Category 5 monster barrels down on the Gulf with the tenacity of a bull staring down a china shop. Chomping at the bit, Julian digs in, ready to destroy, and I intend to fly directly into the maw of Julian's fury. Metaphors aside, things are about to get ugly, and I love every minute of it.

It's been far too long since adrenaline spiked in my veins. After leaving the military, I took a job as a medevac pilot, flying my helicopter to any of the thousands of oil rigs peppered throughout the Gulf.

Dangerous work, injuries are an unfortunate occurrence, despite rigid safety protocols. My crew answers those calls, heading out to ferry the sick and injured back to definitive medical care.

It isn't a kickass job steeped in death and glory, not like the military, but it does have its moments. Most of the time, it's a thankless job, but it pays the bills, and it keeps me flying.

I never feel more alive than with a stick in my hands and air beneath my feet.

This promises to be an interesting run because everyone is headed off the oil rigs rather than flying to them. They flee the storm I willingly fly into.

Pre-flight prep takes most of my concentration, but I think back to the last time I braced for the worst. This is a cake walk compared to that.

My third combat tour in the desert was a shitstorm and ended my career in the Army.

IT WAS EARLY MORNING ON BASE WHEN THE CALL CAME IN. A SPECIAL ops team had injured men on the ground and were pinned down, requesting helicopter evacuation. The area was supposed to be secured by the time my team arrived. After the briefing, my co-pilot, Reggie, aka Rocks, and I went to our helicopter.

The ever-present sand and grit permeated everything. While the team in back secured their gear, Rocks and I went over the flight plan. Once finished, we squeezed the rabbit's foot Rocks hung in the cockpit for good luck. It began our tour gleaming white but was now a dusty brown from all the sand.

"You ready, Angel?" More than a chick who flies, they called me Battle Angel, or Angel for short, a play on a famous Manga character because I was small but packed a punch.

"Ready."

We lifted off and headed into the desert. Fifty clicks out, I dropped down, using the rocky terrain to hide our radar signature.

As we approached our target, gunfire burst from the rocky scree. Pings sounded as bullets struck the outer shell of the helicopter.

"Shit!" The area was supposed to be secure, but it was too hot to land. I piled on speed and began defensive maneuvers as Rocks radioed in a status update.

"They're telling us to leave," he said.

One of the worst parts of the job was aborting a mission and leaving men on the ground, but I couldn't disobey orders. We would return just as soon as it was safe.

As I angled away, a man stood up from behind a large group of rocks with an RPG propped on his shoulder. The man staggered as he fired. A smoke trail headed directly for me bringing a rocket grenade on a direct intercept.

"Evade! Evade! Evade!" I banked hard left, angling down to pick up speed.

Rocks gripped his seat as the helicopter shuddered under the impact. The rocket grenade exploded, taking out the tail section and put me into a spin a hundred and fifty feet off the ground. My entire instrument cluster lit up, lights flashing, alarms blaring.

With deafening alarms screeching in my ears and lights flashing on my display, I fought the deadly spiral.

The helicopter slammed into the ground, crunching and groaning as metal twisted and broke apart. The hard landing bounced us on the rocks and flipped the helicopter on its side.

When I came to, my head felt like it'd been split in two. Smoke poured down my throat. The coppery taint of blood coated my tongue, and I spit out the offensive substance. Blood blurred my vision, but not the macabre scene of Reggie and the shrapnel that speared him through the chest. His eyes stared back at me, filled with the terror of his death. I looked over my shoulder while pulling on the straps securing me to my seat. Two of the SOST team were dead. Two others were injured.

Only after unbuckling did I realize my left leg had been shattered. Smoke filled the air. We were on fire and moments from an explosion. I bit back a scream as I clutched my injured leg and breathed in fumes.

The whole thing was going to blow.

Crawling to the back, I dragged one of the wounded men out of the helicopter, then headed back to rescue the other. A bullet ricocheted off a nearby rock, but I never once thought to stop. I grabbed the last survivor and dragged him toward safety. Bullets peppered the ground around my head, over my shoulders, and beside my hips and my feet. I gave hasty thanks for their terrible aim, at least until one of the shots scored a hit in my good leg.

Gritting my teeth, I dragged the last man behind a sheltering clump of rocks, getting the three of us to safety.

Two years later, my shattered leg and lack of sufficient rehabilitation to make me combat-ready, found me sitting before a medical evaluation board. The Army awarded me a medal and a medical retirement. My military career was over. My career in aviation wasn't, but it was sidelined.

• • •

WE DIDN'T HAVE HURRICANES IN THE DESERT, BUT WE HAD HOSTILES with guns, plenty of ammunition, itchy trigger fingers, and a fanatical will to kill infidels. I battled sandstorms and survived getting shot down. Now, I'm lucky to battle a violent gust or maneuver around a localized storm.

Back then, I flew in hot, hand steady on the stick, with a crew of medics hanging on for dear life with clenched hands and puckered assholes in the back. Landing in the midst of gunfire can make the cockiest pilot quake in their boots or shit their pants, but I faced those kinds of missions with steely determination and eerily cool composure.

I do that now.

A distinguished combat veteran, my hand remains steady as I lift out of Mobile, Alabama, with a critical-care transport team strapped in the back of my helicopter.

Hurricane Julian churns a couple hundred miles offshore, flirting with the western coastline of Florida as it barrels directly toward Mobile. Instead of petering out, it looks to be picking up steam.

Earlier, it looked like any other gorgeous day on the Gulf; deep blue skies with barely any clouds and nearly mirror-smooth waters. The calm before the storm lies about the hell to come.

There are no blue skies for this flight, however. The sun set an hour ago. I fly into the inky blackness and head out to sea.

"It's bumpy as shit back here," Andrew, my flight nurse, calls out through our integrated headsets.

"How's Julian?" Larry, our medic, sounds concerned.

I don't blame him. It's going to be a rough flight, but we're still far ahead of the storm.

I glance at my weather radar. "Still on a direct course."

"How much time?" Larry asks.

"Enough." I try to soothe him, but I'm too busy flying to settle Larry's nerves.

While devastating, hurricanes travel at a relative snail's pace. However, the winds are already kicking up and toss the Gulf into a frenzy. Below us, the normally calm waters churn and the waves kick up. Gusts will make my job harder, but I look forward to the challenge.

"Lots of air traffic," Andrew's voice crackles through the headset.

A glance left confirms Andrew's statement, although it isn't a surprise. Lights from other helicopters dot the night sky as they ferry crew off all active rigs in Julian's path. Beneath us, tossing about in the waves, a steady stream of boat traffic lights up the dark waters.

Flights will continue until all crew members are evacuated from the fixed platforms. Per protocol, stationary rigs evacuate their entire crews, while drillships off-load only non-essential personnel. They then disconnect from their wells and steer the drillship away from the storm to wait things out.

Our patients are on the former, a stationary rig with a complete evacuation underway. Last man off will turn out the lights, as the saying goes. A glance at the clock and I give a nod. We'll have plenty of time to stabilize the wounded crew and make it back far in advance of the worst of the weather. Unfortunately, our helicopter will block the evacuation of the last crewmen remaining.

Hopefully, all non-essential personnel will be gone by the time my crew arrives. The rig I fly toward is located a little more than a hundred miles offshore. We have a relatively quick flight and will be there in thirty to forty-five minutes, depending on changes in wind speed as Julian approaches.

I call the rig, confirm my ETA, and the availability of the landing pad, which gives me twenty minutes to obsess over things I can't control. It'll be nice to have a little more action and pretend the rest of the world doesn't exist.

During the flight, the slow drizzle turns to rain, and the wind kicks up. Hopefully, the heavy stuff is still some distance off. When we approach the rig, I call in and move toward a helideck suspended two hundred feet above a seething sea.

Weather in the Gulf is calm compared to other places around the globe, but I hold a healthy respect for it.

Summers can be pristine without a breath of wind or turn into full-blown squalls within minutes. In the winter, cold fronts move fast, bringing dramatic wind shifts and plummeting temperatures. Fog is more common than not, the result of the high humidity, and of course, there are the ever-present thunderstorms, which crop up with the worst timing, bringing high winds. More than one helicopter has been tossed off a helideck and plunged into the Gulf with those powerful gusts.

My respect isn't healthy. It's profound.

I battle gusts, concerned not only about landing, but a takeoff that threatens to pitch the helicopter into the water below.

It's getting sketchy out here. We won't be able to spend much time on deck, especially with the rain getting heavier. Julian isn't fooling around and picked up speed. It comes to enact a profound vengeance upon the world, and the last thing I want is to be anywhere near the full brunt of its fury.

"Hang on," I call to my passengers. "It's going to be bumpy, and don't unbuckle until I tell you."

Understandably, the flight nurse and paramedic are eager to get to our patients, but if they get out before the skids are anchored, it could be the last thing they do. Before touching down, I arm the floats, a precaution in case I don't stick the landing. If the gusts buck us off the platform, the floats will deploy, giving us a chance of escaping the helicopter. My motto is to plan for the worst and pray for the best.

Right now, I wish for a break in the sheets of rain pouring down. I can't see crap.

Almost there.

A gust blows me off the helideck and I curse. This is turning into a real goat rope. But I regain altitude and realign for a second approach. Winds gust from the southeast, Julian testing the waters.

Okay, easy now. There's a flare boom to the right and a crane to the left I need to avoid. I kick the tail a little to the right after clearing a stairwell. One more check to make sure the floats are armed.

Holy crap! Where did that antenna come from?

Hands steady, I clear the antenna and make a note to speak to their Offshore Installation Manager about putting stuff up above the deck level. The skids touch down, and I radio an update back to base. The whine of the engine powers down, and the rotors come to a stop.

In the back, Andrew and Larry gather our gear, hefting packs to their backs and ready the stretchers. They wait for me to give the all-clear.

Outside, three men wait. Shrouded in rain gear, their bulky orange shapes flash in the landing lights. Beneath their hoods, their faces fall into shadow.

I spent eight years in the military. Alpha men are a dime a dozen in the Army, but we all had the same purpose, the same mission. The business of oil drilling attracts a similar breed, rough and rugged men, only these don't hold to a code I understand. With the military, everyone marches to the same drummer, follows the same orders, and can be trusted implicitly.

Drillers? They're a rough lot.

They make me uncomfortable, and I don't trust them.

Gusts buffet the helideck and the craft shudders. As the whine of the engine disappears, another sound replaces it. A deep, thunderous booming, felt more than heard, joins the roar of the wind. Vibrations from waves crashing against the support pillars rip through the super-structure. Nature's power literally shakes the world.

I pop open my door and signal to the waiting crew it's safe to approach. They rush forward and secure my skids, bracing the helicopter against the rising winds. They do the same to the rotors overhead.

Once the skids are locked securely to the helideck, I give the signal for Andrew and Larry. The two men jump out, packs strapped to their backs and portable stretchers in tow.

This isn't our first foray to one of the thousands of oil rigs distributed throughout the Gulf. The imposing structures never fail to inspire awe, and I feel some of that now pounding in my blood. Or maybe that's adrenaline spiking along my nerves? It doesn't matter. Everything about this situation is intense.

Safety protocols have been drilled into me, as they have for my crew. Many of the walkways, stairwells, and ladders span vast distances with deadly drops beneath them. One hand on the rail at all times. It's a mantra we live with. A fall here can be fatal. Drilling remains one of the most dangerous professions for a reason.

A thick arm braces my door as a gust tries to slam it shut on my leg.

"Careful!" a gruff voice shouts.

"Thanks."

He pulls back, a look of surprise on his face. "You're a chick."

"All day. Every day."

"Huh." He holds the door open against the wind. "Come with me."

"I'll stay here, thank you."

"Not happening. Too dangerous." His gruff features brook no argument as he studies my face. An aura of authority surrounds him and slams into me with the absolute assurance I will do as he says.

My entire career has been spent facing down dominant men and overcoming male and female stereotypes that define who I can and can't be. I earned my right to pilot the helicopter and won't let his overwhelming presence force me into feeling less because I happen to be a chick.

But that authoritative aura?

It does things—spins my thoughts, teases my mind, and draws forth a powerful need to cave to his demands. To dispel the effect he has on me, I shake my head and grit my teeth.

"I'm staying with the helicopter."

"No. You're not." He props open the door, leans in, and pulls me out of my seat.

Chapter Two

Aiden

I CAN'T BELIEVE MY EYES WHEN I SEE WHO LANDS THE HELICOPTER IN the middle of the storm.

A female?

Women are few and far between out on the rigs, but female pilots are even rarer. As if that isn't enough, this one appears to be stubborn as shit, refusing to comply with my commands.

Doesn't she know who's in charge around here?

"Let go of me." Her tiny hand pounds against my chest.

I don't mean to frighten her, only to get her off the platform. It isn't safe to stay with the helicopter, not with the gusts we're seeing.

If she was a man, it wouldn't be an issue. I would have yanked a man out and kicked his ass all the way to the ladder leading to the catwalk. I don't take lip from any of my crew, and definitely not from those unfamiliar with how things work on a rig.

All I care about is safety.

What I don't need is to carry on a long, drawn-out conversation about what should be a non-issue. The helideck isn't safe, and there is no way in hell I'll leave anybody, man or woman, alone up here in this weather. I release the pilot and point to the stairs. Maybe she'll listen to reason.

"No need to get your panties in a wad, but get your ass down those stairs." I cross my arms over my chest. The orange survival suit squeaks as it strains across my bulky chest.

"Why you … you …" Her face turns beet red.

I shouldn't laugh. I really should hold it together, but I can't help myself. A low chuckle escapes me.

"Let me help you out. Asshole, brute, dickhead?" A grin plasters itself on my face, and I can't make it go away. She looks so damn indignant and sexy as hell. "Which one is it going to be?"

"You're a prick," she says with a huff, "you know that?"

"Ah, I hadn't gotten to prick yet, but it is next."

I glance into the darkness. The sea seethes below us. The waves are double in size from earlier in the day. This hurricane is going to pack a punch, and if we don't hurry things along, we won't make it off the rig before all hell breaks loose.

I turn my attention to the pretty pilot. "Look, I get that you want to stay with the helicopter, but it's not safe. Therefore, it's not happening."

"It's not safe crawling around a rig in the dark either. I'll take my chances."

"Not happening."

I reach for her, but she jerks away and crosses her arms over her chest. I can't help the way my eyes drop to take in the curve of her breasts. The defiant stare she levels at me makes me grin.

This chick has a temper. I respect that. But I'm still in charge.

Too many women cave beneath my demands. Frankly, I find it boring, but this hellcat sparks my interest and stimulates other parts of my anatomy, which have no business taking notice … at least not now.

"And what are you going to do about it?"

Her defiance stirs something deep inside, something primal and highly inappropriate. I can't help it, needing to see how far she will take this. By rights, she has no choice but to follow my orders. As the Offshore Installation Manager, I'm the final authority on the rig, but then maybe she doesn't understand how things work out here? I'll have to break it to her because she can't refuse one of my orders.

"Get out of that helicopter and follow me down, or I'll toss you over my shoulder and carry you. Since I have a feeling you'll kick and scream, and knowing I need to keep a hand on a railing at all times, that won't end well for either of us. I don't know about you, but I'd rather not dump you over the railing. There are sharks in these waters."

"A fall from this height is fatal," she says.

"You'd still be shark bait. How about we skip feeding the sharks and you do as you're told? What's it going to be? You coming with me? Or do I have to carry you?" I size her up, thinking about how much fun that can be.

"There's no way in hell you're carrying me. I'll bring you up on assault charges." She edges away from me.

"I respect that." I mirror her pose and stare down at her. "But you're not filing charges. I'm the only one in charge around here, which means you do as I say."

"Bossy much?"

"You have no idea." With a sweep of my arm, I gesture toward the stairs. "Ladies choice: on your feet or over my shoulder? I can tell you which one I prefer, but that might get me written up."

"You're an ass. You know that?"

"I'm also a stickler for safety and for others following my orders." I stretch out my hand. "I'm Aiden Cole, OIM, that means Offshore Installation …."

"I know what an OIM is, asshole."

Her temper and sharp comebacks are sexy as fuck. Despite the dangerous conditions, impending superstorm, and the very real threat of having to ride out the storm on the rig, she turns me on. None of that is good.

"Good, then you know you have to do as I say."

"I don't see why I can't stay here."

As if to support my argument, the wind whips over the helideck and nearly blows off the door to the helicopter. I grab it, stabilizing it until the gust dies down.

Her eyes widen as the helicopter rocks in the clamps. It's locked tight and won't be going anywhere, but that was one hell of a gust. With Julian approaching, things will only get worse.

"Look, it's going to take a moment to stabilize my crewmen. Then we have to load them on stretchers, walk them back, and lift them from that deck down there to this one up here. There's only the five of us left on this rig, and I'm not leaving anyone alone where I don't have eyes on them."

The play of emotions marching across her face is interesting to watch. I'm not kidding about tossing her over my shoulder. It isn't an exaggeration and will be highly unsafe, but she seems to believe I might do just that. Which has me considering what it'll feel like to drape her over my shoulder and go all caveman on her, and that has me thinking about how much fun it could be to tie her to my bed and do other things.

With a shake of my head, I toss the fantasy and focus on maintaining my professionalism. She makes that impossible, however, with her brown, doe eyes and pert little mouth.

With a huff, she exits the helicopter. Poor thing is barely five-foot-six and looks like she weighs a buck twenty at most. The slightest gust could sweep her off the decking.

"Stay here." I grip her hand and place it over the handle of the door, indicating she should hang on.

"I thought I was supposed to go with you."

"You are, but you need a harness."

"Andrew and Larry didn't need harnesses."

"They're also well over two hundred pounds. You're half that, and I'll be damned if I let the medevac pilot get blown off the platform."

"I'm not going to—"

Another gust sweeps over the rig. Metal groans and it slams her against the helicopter. If the wind had come from the other direction, she would've been knocked to her ass and would've slid halfway across the deck. Her grip tightens and she gives a clipped nod.

Finally, some sense settles into her head. I go to a utility box and retrieve a safety harness. I already wear one, as do my men. Before we make our way back, I'll need to make sure the transport team have them as well.

Is it even safe to take off in weather like this?

I don't know, but the pilot doesn't seem concerned. That's a good thing because no one wants to ride out a hurricane trapped inside a rig. I sure don't, but will the company send another helicopter to pick up my remaining crewmen?

It's already on its way, but the timing is going to be tight. I need to get my wounded off the rig before that helicopter can land and evacuate the last of my men.

Gritting my teeth, I return to the pilot with the webbing. Not caring what she thinks about where I might or might not be touching, I force her to step into the harness and pull it up to her waist. Tightening the straps, I hook one end of a short strap to a D-ring on her harness and fasten the other end to mine. Now, at least if the wind tries to blow her away, she'll be anchored to me.

I give another smirk, thinking about tying her down again.

"You ready?" I have to shout to be heard over the wind.

Unlike me, she doesn't have weather gear. Rain drips down her face, but her tight bun keeps her hair out of the way. I bet a million dollars this chick is prior military with that tight-ass regulation bun. It makes more sense, to be honest.

She gives a nod and I head toward the stairs. It's a bit of a hike from the helideck down the stairs and across catwalks to the crew area. I have two men in the sickbay. One with multiple leg fractures and the other is knocked out cold.

The accident occurred when the men rushed to tie down equipment in advance of the storm. Rushing and a momentary lack of attention were all it took for an accident to happen.

I lead the way, pointing to the railings she needs to grip as we go up and down stairs and across the catwalks. The woman listens as I bark orders, obeying immediately.

Yeah, she's prior military.

Despite the noise from the growling winds, the rig sits in silence. Shut down, it's prepped to hunker down and endure the storm. It'll take a massive storm to upset the rig, but the company doesn't take chances with its men. Everyone is evacuated until the storm passes.

We move by a row of emergency lifeboats: red torpedoes which hang over the ocean. In the event of an emergency, they release and plummet down to the water over two hundred feet below. I pray to never have to take that ride. The company says it is safe, but I doubt it.

Unsinkable, they can endure any storm. The occupants inside, however, will be tossed about like corks. Without any orientation as to up and down, and with no view of the outside world, they'll all come out covered in one another's vomit. I've never been in one and might choose going down with the rig over climbing into one of those. That decision will be mine to make, but I have faith in my rig. It won't fail me.

"Come on. It's just a bit further."

The woman is a fighter. She struggles with the wind. Head down, white-knuckled grip, and soaked to the bone, she doesn't voice one word of complaint.

Yet another thing I admire.

The door to the crew area is just ahead and I lead her to it as fast as safety allows. It's getting dicey outside.

I yank on the door, then hold it open. She steps under my arm and over the hatchway. I follow her inside and remove my safety gear. With a turn of the locking mechanism, I seal us away from the storm and the howling wind. It seems eerily quiet inside, and I'm suddenly hyperaware of the beautiful woman trembling beside me.

Her teeth chatter and she looks like a ghost.

"We need to get you into something dry."

"W-wh-where are m-m-my m-men?"

"Darlin', your teeth are chattering so hard I can barely understand a word you're saying."

Her gaze pops to mine and determination flashes in their depths. "Where are they?"

I point down the hall. "Not far."

She turns and stomps down the hallway. Guess we're going to sickbay.

Chapter Three

Ariel

MY HEART HAMMERS IN MY CHEST AND I CAN BARELY BREATHE. I tell myself it has nothing to do with the imposing stranger walking behind me, although he's a sight to melt the coldest heart.

Tall, imposing, stunningly attractive, his baby blues stop me in my tracks. Baby blues are my Achilles heel, and I've fallen for them one time too many.

But that's not why my heart races.

From the very first step on the stairs leading down from the helideck, terror holds me in its iron-fisted grip. Thankfully, I have the OIM's broad shoulders to stare at as he leads the way. It helps to keep my attention from straying from the rails of the catwalks to the deadly depths they span. Beneath them, an angry sea surges as white-capped waves slam against the support pillars of the oil rig.

As the OIM moves me from one catwalk to another, the blood in my veins races inside my body with the same ferocity as the wind buffeting me outside.

As a helicopter pilot, height isn't something I fear. How many times have I stared between my feet, watching the ground drop away? Or how about all the times I willingly rappelled out of a helicopter?

I live most of my life between ground level and five thousand feet. I've conquered any number of fears in life, survived the heat of battle, and I've never been afraid.

That roiling sea, with its unrestrained fury? It makes me feel small, inconsequential, and terribly vulnerable.

The fear running rampant in my body must be a combination of the wind, the darkness, and the driving rain, which makes me grit my teeth and struggle to take the next step. Rain soaks the thick fabric of my flight suit, and the wind chills me to the bone. My teeth chatter and my hands shake.

Hypothermia much?

That walk takes less than five minutes, yet I arrive in the throes of a full-bodied shiver. I have to walk back the way I came, and it won't be quick. Not with two stretchers to maneuver. How am I going to fly when I can barely control my hands?

"Take the hall to your left." He speaks in one of those sexy Texan drawls, and the way his eyes spark when he laughs makes my belly flutter. I don't need to deal with school girl infatuation and decide I need to stay far away from this man.

"Second left, and then take the first door on your right."

He guides me, keeping pace as I stomp down the halls. Why am I angry? There's no reason to be this pissed off at a guy who's merely doing his job.

It isn't him.

It's my reaction to him.

The one thing in life I abhor is not being in control, and he stole all my self-control the moment those baby blues of his breached my defenses. He reminds me of a disaster of a man, one who took my heart and shredded it to pieces.

I take in a deep breath and force myself to calm down. At least I know what stirs my anger. Except for the drawl, he's a dead ringer for Rick, the last disaster in a string of failed relationships with blue-eyed men.

"Thanks."

I feel a little calmer after that cleansing breath. Maybe another one, two, or four will help? Now that I know why the OIM triggered such a strong reaction, I can do something to counteract it.

At least, that's the plan.

I open the door the OIM indicates and step inside. Andrew and Larry are already hard at work, leaning over two men stretched out on two gurneys. Their injuries weren't a part of my pre-flight brief, but I listened in on the two men during the flight. There was an accident that crushed one of the men and knocked the other one unconscious.

"How's it looking, guys?" I glance between them, admiring their efficiency.

Andrew looks up. "ABCs on this one are stable, but the breaks are bad."

Airway, breathing, and circulation; those are the basics of first aid. I was trained in Buddy Care in the military and know enough to put someone into the recovery position and how to stop most bleeding.

"Can I help?"

"I've got a good pulse in both feet, but he shattered his legs." Andrew turns back to his patient.

"Just tell me what to do."

With adrenaline kicking in, all thoughts of being cold move from my mind. I rub my hands together, bringing warmth back to my icy fingers, and crouch down on the other side of Andrew's patient.

"Help me with the splint, then we'll get him loaded on the stretcher."

"Gotcha."

"What can we do?" the OIM asks.

He mentioned his name, but I can't for the life of me remember what it is. What I do remember is everything else he said, things about tossing me over his shoulder and … I blink hard and force those thoughts from my mind.

The OIM squats beside me and I can't focus on what Andrew says.

"Help Ariel," Andrew instructs. "Support his leg while I put on the brace. It's hard to tell if his pelvis is fractured, but it looks like it might be. It's going to be tricky getting him on the stretcher. I've given him all the pain meds I dare. Doesn't look like there are any other injuries." Andrew glances at me. "It looks pretty bad out there. What are your thoughts about flying out?"

I purse my lips. "It's going to be dicey, to be sure. I'll need to check the wind speed before we take off. The book answer is safety takeoff limits are set at forty knots, but I've been out in fifty-five. Not sure I want to take off in much more than that."

"What does that mean?" The OIM levels his powerful gaze at me, making me gulp. "Can you leave or not?"

Ignoring those mesmerizing eyes, I force myself to swallow against the lump in my throat. It's the only way to silence the fluttering in my belly.

"Winds are pegging forty right now. It's going to be dicey, and those gusts are only going to intensify. Obviously, the sooner we get loaded, the better."

Larry looks up from placing an intravenous line in his patient. "This one is also stable. Large knot on his skull. Not sure what's going on in his head. Concussion for certain, but it might be worse. How far out is the hurricane?"

"Last I looked, 150 nautical miles." I turn to address the OIM and am determined to treat him like any other Joe. They're just eyes. "Where's your weather station?"

Penetrating, mesmerizing, incredibly blue eyes. There's something about him that makes me tremble.

Separated from the helicopter, I no longer have access to my weather radar or communication back to base.

"Not far," the OIM says. "I can take you there if you want."

I purse my lips. "I can push a takeoff to sixty-knot winds. It's ill-advised, but I'm thinking hanging out here is a worse option."

"The rig hasn't sunk yet. It's endured hurricanes before," he says.

"A Category 5?" I ask.

"Well, we don't get those much in the Gulf, but yeah, it's withstood one or two."

"Hmm, I don't think we want to get out there only to find out we can't take off." I scrunch my brows. "Where's your ride?"

"Inbound behind you. These guys are our priority. Once you leave, our ride will land and take us out."

I shake my head. "Honestly, I don't see that happening. The gusts we're getting are already bad. If they're on their way, it's best if they head back to base." I glance at his other two crewmen who haven't yet said a word and do some quick math in my head. "I don't have the weight allowance to take all of you, but I can take one, maybe two if we offload some gear."

"Duncan and Randall can go with you. I'll hunker down here."

That's impressive. It didn't take him a second to make that decision.

I respect that, but then I have a thing for men who take charge, especially in the bedroom. Some say it's an unhealthy obsession. Next to blue eyes, men who wear authority like a second skin are a surefire path to my destruction. I should add that to the growing list of reasons to stay far away from this one.

"I'm sorry," I say. "I'd take everyone if I could."

"You can't change the law of physics. Don't worry about me. I've seen worse than a simple storm."

Holy rocking that confidence.

Blue eyes, authority, self-assuredness? He hits all my buttons. I respond too, dry mouth, lump in throat, and butterflies in my stomach, which refuse to sit still.

Get a grip.

The OIM and I hold the splint in place while Andrew secures it around the injured man's leg. Once that's done, I'm shivering again.

"How does it look, Andrew?" I glance at Andrew and the deep-set scowl on his face.

"It'll do. Maybe another fifteen minutes to get them loaded on the stretchers."

That will give me enough time to check on the weather. I stand and take a step back. Mr. OIM rises with me.

"You ready to check it out?" Did his drawl thicken in the past five minutes?

I close my mouth. I was staring at the prominent bulge in his pants. "Excuse me?"

"The weather radar?" He arches a brow, then checks me out, letting his gaze linger on my tits.

As cold as I am, my nipples harden into rocks beneath my flight suit. Thank goodness he can't see them. I would be mortified if he knew.

"You're shivering." His tone softens. "Can't let that happen. Need you to fly everyone out. We need to get you into something dry."

Right, while leaving him behind. Alone to sit out the storm.

"You know, if we went to the helicopter, I could try to dump more weight. I might be able to get all of us back to shore."

"I appreciate that." He pauses. "More than you know, but you saw what it's like out there. No way can we lighten that helicopter safely. Best we make sure you can take off and take it from there."

"Okay, it's just …"

He bends down to look me in the eye.

"Sugar, I'll be fine. It'll be rough, but this place is built for this shit. Won't be my first rodeo."

"How long do you think it'll take to get them to the helideck?"

"It's not going to be easy. Twenty minutes maybe?"

"Okay. I guess we have time to show me your radar."

"Sure, luv. Let's go take a look at my radar."

I pause, then crack a smile when he gives me a wink.

Humor too? This man has it all.

I wave to Andrew. "I'll be back in a minute."

Andrew has the OIM's other two crewmen setting up the stretchers. They should be ready to go by the time I get back.

Chapter Four

Aiden

I DON'T MISS THE SPARK WHICH FLASHES IN THE PRETTY PILOT'S EYES. If we were anywhere else, I know exactly how the evening would end—my place or hers with twisted sheets beneath us.

As it is, all hell is about to break loose as Hurricane Julian slams into us.

She wants to look at the radar, gauge wind speed, and decide whether to fly out of this shitstorm. I can't believe she'll even consider it. Hell, I thought she was crazy to land on the helideck.

As it is, I respect any decision she makes. She's the only qualified individual to fly that helicopter, which means only she can determine if it's safe to take off.

But she'll be taking four of my men with her, two of whom are injured. If I think for a minute their lives will be in greater danger in that helicopter rather than hunkering down on the rig, words will be exchanged between me and the pilot.

A short trip through the crew quarters brings us to what functions as a control center. I hold the door open and let her step inside.

"Weather radar is over there." The rig has a fully functional weather station on board.

Ariel doesn't waste any time. She familiarizes herself with the controls, then sets to it. I stand silently while she pulls up information on the path of the storm, its speed, wind velocities, and whatever else she needs. Meanwhile, I stare out the windows as they rattle and shake with the advance of the storm.

Hurricane Julian isn't fooling around. It isn't supposed to hit for another couple of hours, but it seems like it's far ahead of schedule. Hurricanes have been known to slow down as they approach land, and I hope Julian chooses to do that. It will increase the chances of getting my men off the rig and home to safety.

Keeping my thoughts to myself, I plan for every contingency. If we get stuck, I need to find the best place for everyone to shelter. Someplace protected from the worst of the winds, unlikely to be damaged during the storm, yet close enough to the emergency lifeboats in case the unthinkable happens.

Not that anything will happen to the rig. It was built to withstand the storm of the century and then some.

"Shit!" Ariel punches the screen. "Shit! Shit! Double Shit!"

The girl has a mouth on her.

"That doesn't sound reassuring." I turn and cross my arms over my chest.

As if it were possible, her anger only makes her more attractive. I love the way her tiny fists punch the screen and the way her lips twist in frustration. A spitfire attitude promises many things in more intimate surroundings, but then again, I've always been a man who enjoys aggressive, private play.

I really shouldn't be thinking about sex, but she makes that damn near impossible. Not with the flashing of anger in her eyes, that tight body the flight suit does nothing to hide, or the fierceness she brings to her job. Everything about her screams sex.

"It's a total clusterfuck." She kicks the console. "That's what this is."

"Such words from a lady," I tease, trying to keep the mood light. "My ears are burning."

She spins around and cocks her hip forward. Sparks ignite in her eyes, and I can almost see the steam coming out of her ears. "I'm pretty sure my language is the least offensive thing you've heard all week."

"True, but I have to say, you'd give the men a run for their money with that filthy mouth of yours. Good thing we don't have a swear jar around here." I unclasp my arms and lean against the counter.

"You're kidding, right?" She glances left and right, searching.

I can't help but grin. In a place like this, we need a swear barrel, and it would be filled to the brim daily.

"One thing you'll discover about me is that I seldom kid," I say. "Fortunately, we don't have one here. Consider yourself safe."

She seems to consider my words and I wonder if her thoughts travel down any of the filthy paths I've already taken ten times over.

"I bet," she says. "You'd all be broke."

A sense of humor. I like that.

I give a laugh. "True, but I do have one at home." Let her extrapolate from that.

"I'm guessing the wife doesn't appreciate swearing around the kids?"

Uh-oh, that's a wrong turn.

I don't need her thinking I'm unavailable. Truth is, it's been a long time since I've dated, but I'm definitely unencumbered. Time to steer her in the right direction, but I need to make sure she understands certain things. Surprises like mine aren't generally accepted well. If my daughter is going to be a deal-breaker, best to know up front. It's time to test the waters.

"When my nine-year-old spouted out *cunt motherfucker*, I knew something had to change."

She places her hand to her mouth and laughs. "Oh my, that is a mouthful for a boy."

"Well, I guess *she* wanted to be like her old man."

"A girl?" Her laughter spills through the room. "Now that's priceless. I bet you need a swear jar, and I bet your daughter is the richest nine-year-old in the neighborhood."

"That might not be far off from the truth. It's most definitely not my finest parenting moment."

"I bet your wife was pissed. Of all the words for a girl to hear, let alone repeat ..."

"Yeah, I got an earful, but not from the Missus." One of the reasons I don't date, other than working on an oil rig two weeks out of every month, is because I spend every minute of my time ashore with my kid.

"You're kidding, right?"

"I meant to say there is no Missus. Just me, Callie and Jewels, her pet iguana."

"An iguana? I expected a dog or cat for a girl, or a fluffy hamster, not a salmonella-infested reptile."

"Well, Callie isn't like most girls, and I'm surprised you'd stereotype considering what you do for a living." My comment seems to give her pause.

She gives me a look. "So, are you divorced or ...?"

Her question holds more than casual interest. I'm willing to feed her interest; I'm interested in her but will begin with the truth first. Best to get that shit out of the way at the start.

"Widowed." One of those gut-wrenching twists grabs me in the gut. It never gets easier, but I made a promise to my late wife that I would honor her dying wish no matter how impossible it seems. "A little over eight years."

"I'm sorry." She places a hand over her heart.

"Don't be. I had a great marriage. We had Callie, and I have the best memories."

"How did ..." She seems hesitant to ask the question polite conversation demands.

I'm not going to leave her hanging. I've had years to get over Samantha's death. It's far past time to move on. I made a promise I haven't kept and something about this pilot tells me it might be time to rectify that.

"Breast cancer, the aggressive kind. They found cancer when Sam was pregnant. Already aggressive, there were few options—start chemo and lose the baby, or wait and deal with it after. Sam didn't hesitate, even knowing what delaying treatment would most likely mean." The cancer ate at Samantha's body while she nurtured our growing daughter in her womb. "Chemotherapy started after Callie's delivery, but it was too late. The cancer was too advanced."

"Aiden..." Samantha's voice trailed off. Too weak to speak, she tried nonetheless.

"Shh, you don't have to say a word."

"I know."

All the color had left her face. I stared down at her pale complexion and the wan smile she struggled to keep for me. Such a trooper, she remained strong until the end.

"I ..." Weakness pulled at her, and she closed her eyes.

I brushed the hair back from her face and kissed her forehead. "You don't have to say it. I love you too." I knew what she wanted to say but couldn't bear the heartbreak it would bring. Sam wanted me to move on, but I wouldn't. I couldn't.

Too frail to move, her fingers twitched on the starched hospital sheets. I took her hand in mine and rubbed the pad of my thumb over the thin, crepe-like skin and spider veins. Her eyes pinched with pain. Relentless in its attack, the cancer settled into her bones, bringing unrelenting pain.

"How's Callie?"

Our daughter was born a beautiful and perfect little thing and was just a few months old but already bursting with personality. Callie would never know her mother.

"She's with your mom. Do you want to see her?"

Babies weren't allowed in the intensive care unit, although the staff made exceptions for the dying mother. My mother-in-law sat with Callie in the waiting room and would bring her when the time came. It wouldn't be long. Samantha would be released from her burdens soon.

"I do, but I want to talk to you ..."

I didn't want to hear it. She was going to say goodbye and then something much worse.

"I want you to promise ..."

I threaded my fingers through hers as my heart cracked and broke apart.

"Sam, I can't ..."

She shook her head. "Promise ..."

This wasn't the first time she asked me to give my word, but how could I promise the impossible?

"Sam ..."

Her words gutted me from the inside out, and I couldn't swallow past my grief. I would live my life without the love of my life and raise our child alone. Not fully alone; Samantha's mother already promised to help me raise her granddaughter.

I wasn't ready. I never would be. There was no future without Samantha.

"You deserve happiness."

There would be no joy without her, no happiness, and nobody else. I couldn't conceive of loving another. I held her hand while tears spilled down my cheeks.

"You've given me everything, Sam. Love I never imagined possible and the most beautiful baby girl in the world. I'm happy."

"Aiden, that's not enough. I won't let you mourn me for the rest of your life. I want you to live and love again."

"I have Callie. I'm happy. I don't need anything else."

"I know the kind of man you are. You're too wonderful not to share your love with another. You deserve love."

I didn't want to talk about another woman. It felt too much like cheating, and I wouldn't consider the idea, not with my wife dying in my arms, but it seemed important to Sam.

She needed my promise before she could let go, and hell if she hadn't fought long enough. It was selfish to deny her dying wish.

I brought her hand to my mouth and pressed my lips to the paper-thin skin. The cancer stole Sam's strength and destroyed the woman I loved.

"I promise." Tears ran down my face with a promise I never planned on keeping.

She breathed out a sigh and her expression eased of all its pain. Her fingers fluttered in my palm. The beeping on the monitors slowed.

"Mr. Cole ..." A nurse stepped into my wife's room. "It's time."

"Can you get my mother-in-law?" I wouldn't leave Sam's side, but her mother needed to be here.

"Of course." The nurse left and brought my mother-in-law and Callie into the room.

Callie's soft coos sounded and she blew raspberries while her mother took her last breath. I held my wife's hand while Samantha died, knowing I would never love another.

"You don't have to talk about it," Ariel says in a rush.

My knuckles turn white with the death grip I have on the counter, and my cheeks are wet with tears. I swipe at my cheeks, angry and embarrassed by the rare show of emotion.

"Sorry about that. It never gets easier."

"I didn't mean to bring up bad memories." The pilot holds out her palm and places it against my chest.

Such a simple, comforting gesture, I don't know how to react. I'm used to being the strong one, not an emotional tear bag. It isn't the best way to impress a woman, but whatever, I can shed a tear or two for my dead wife.

"Sam isn't a bad memory. She was an amazing mother and a wonderful wife who wished for nothing more than for her husband to live a full life."

Now I'm rhyming? Can this get any worse?

I hope Ariel understands what I'm getting at. The air crackles between us, an attraction that can't be denied. I've never felt anything like this before. It's as if I've been struck by lightning and the pilot is at the center of it all.

Samantha made me promise I would move on. I haven't, but that's only because there hasn't been a woman smart enough, strong enough, or tenacious enough to hold my interest. I've known this woman less than an hour and my skin hasn't stopped buzzing.

Ariel's smile returns. "She sounds like an amazing person, but I think *cunt* might not be the best word to teach your daughter."

She doesn't shy away from curse words, either. Many women find the word *cunt* highly offensive, but the word practically rolls off her dirty tongue.

I like that.

I let out a deep belly laugh. Even better than her filthy mouth, she has no problem calling me out on my bad language.

I love it.

"Now, that's great advice. Which is where the swear jar comes in. Callie makes a fortune off my little slip-ups."

"I bet she does." Ariel spins around. "As for us, motherfucking cunt is a pretty apt description of our situation."

"Doesn't look good?"

Damn, the woman switches gears without missing a beat. I haven't had a chance to work anything else in before she goes all professional on me.

"Wind speeds are gusting at fifty knots. I could take off, but by the time we get your guys loaded on the helicopter, wind speeds will be far in excess of that. Julian has stepped up its game. It's not worth the risk. We're grounded until this blows over."

"We should probably tell the others."

"You go do that. I'm going to find out about your ride. They need to turn back if they haven't already."

"Did you forget about me not leaving anyone alone?"

She gestures to the room. "Where exactly do you think I'm going? I'm not heading out for a stroll, and I think I can find my way back. For the record, you left the rest of them alone."

"For ex-military, you're not that good at following orders." I watch for the slightest reaction, wondering how I should play this.

"Sorry, didn't know that was a command, sir."

Her deliciously brown eyes darken as her pupils dilate. And I don't miss the way she licks her lips. Is it possible she feels the energy sizzling between us too?

"Say that again." I take a step toward her.

She takes a step back but is stopped short by the console. I take another step, and she grips the edge of the counter but doesn't move away.

I level my entire focus on her eyes, holding her with the force of my will. Her chin juts forward. She gulps and licks those damn lips again.

"Say what?" A quiver bounces in her voice.

"You know what I mean."

I take another step. Only a few inches separate us. Over six feet tall, I tower over her small frame. Now is the time for her to step to the side, but she doesn't.

She holds my stare, then drops her gaze as I lean slightly forward.

"Do you like bossy men?"

"That depends on the man and where we are." Her words come as a breathy whisper. "It's also important he's not an asshole."

"Is that so?" I itch to touch her but will wait until there's no doubt as to whether she wants more.

"Are you an asshole?"

Damn, but her words set my blood on fire.

"I'm not an asshole. I have a little girl to raise and have very specific ideas on how women should be treated ... depending where we are."

I toss her words back at her, gauging her interest and whether I read her right.

Her gasp tells me everything I need to know.

"Although, I run a tight ship, or rather, a tight rig. I can be a certified asshole if the safety of my men is compromised."

Her gaze bounces to my eyes, but she doesn't hold it for long before dipping her chin and biting at her lip.

"I'm wondering what you're going to do." I lean in, crowding her space.

"What do you mean?"

"When I kiss you ..."

Her eyes widen, and her lips part ever so slightly.

"You'll understand why when I do."

Words aren't necessary for what comes next, and screw professionalism.

A Category 5 hurricane barrels down on us. We'll be stuck in close quarters with the others until the infernal storm blows over or sinks the rig. It makes no sense not to go for it, and I'm long past ignoring the electricity crackling between us.

I wrap a hand around her waist and pull her to me. I really should ask permission, but the hand she places on my chest doesn't push away. Her fingers curl in my shirt and tug. When I pull her close, my body roars with its need to possess, but this isn't something I intend to rush.

No, I'll savor the moment, drawing it out until she begs for contact. I glide my hand up the nape of her neck and slide it over the perfection of the tight bun at the back of her head. I look at her in a way I haven't looked at any woman since my darling Samantha passed away.

Ariel's eyes glitter in the overhead lights. Sparks of passion and lustful desire flash as a teasing smile creeps across her face.

Samantha made me promise to move on and open my heart to the possibility of loving again. I haven't been able to honor her dying wish.

Until now.

With the demands of work and raising my daughter alone, there simply hasn't been the time to date. I could've frequented any strip club and slaked my physical ache, but that isn't the kind of woman I desire.

I need confident and self-assured; a woman strong enough to allow herself to be vulnerable and yet willing to yield to a man like me.

The acceleration of my heart is a blend of everything my body wants, mixed with a tinge of fear. The desire in Ariel's eyes can't be ignored. It mirrors mine.

No hesitation.

No guilt.

With a gentle press of my finger, I lift her chin, tilting her face to meet my gaze. The passion brimming in her eyes, that hot intensity, is all the permission I need to ignite the inferno to come.

The rest of the world becomes unimportant. The storm outside fades into insignificance, and the men down the hall disappear. Everything but Ariel is banished into the far recesses of my mind.

The heat of her breath brushes against my skin, but I don't rush.

This is a moment to savor. A nearly impossible task, I ignore the stirring within me. My desire is a caged beast that has been contained for far too long. It struggles to be free. The only thing that matters is touching her more.

I would try to be gentle but know I'll fail. I cup her cheek with one hand while freeing the long lengths from the bun at the back of her head. She shivers as I shake out the wet lengths of her hair. I lean in and feather my thumb against her lower lip, demanding she open for me. Completely in tune with my need, she parts her lips and swipes her tongue along my thumb.

"Do that again." Deep, raw, and hoarse with tightly held restraint, I give the command.

Her eyes close, and a curtain of dark lashes sweeps over her high cheekbones. She presses the tip of her tongue to my thumb, then sucks my thumb into her mouth. The warmth of her mouth makes me groan with need.

Her eyes open and she stares at me through those thick lashes. I weave my fingers through her hair. Pulling her head back, I pull my thumb free of the wet heat of her mouth.

I want to take the zipper of her flight suit and yank it down, but we are still in the *getting to know you* stage. She reaches up and grips my neck, pulling me down while she rises up on her toes.

I yank on her hair, a firm tug to let her know I'm in charge and give a satisfied nod at her frustrated whimper. She holds her hands around my neck but no longer tries to force the kiss. I don't make her wait long, needing to feel her lips on me. Leaning down, I close the distance.

Demanding and determined, I don't take time to coax a response from her. I plunder and plunge, taking what I want.

Her fingers lose their grip around my neck and slide down my chest, clutching at my shirt. Her entire body seems to melt into me as I swirl my tongue against hers.

Long dormant nerves stir to life, hardening me in an instant. My entire body seems to come alive with a riot of sensation as desire ignites into an unslakable thirst for more.

I rock my body against hers, allowing her to feel the boldness of my erection pressed between us. That will come later, but it will happen. An inevitability exists between us, and I determine then that I will pursue this woman.

For the first time ever, honoring Samantha's wish feels like the right thing to do.

Chapter Five

Ariel

A TOE-CURLING, HEART-STOPPING, SOUL-TINGLING WAVE OF sensation sweeps down my body with the unapologetic ferocity of a single kiss.

His name? What is his name?

He mentioned it, but for the life of me, I can't remember the name of the man kissing me. Hell, I can barely remember to breathe.

The kiss overwhelms nearly every thought in my head. Delicious. Sensual. Arousing.

Long-slumbering parts of my anatomy wake up and take notice. This isn't something I've ever felt before.

He has me by the waist and pulls me hard against him. There's no denying the rock-hard prominence pressed against my belly. The swell of his arousal is thick, hard, and persistent.

What the hell am I doing? Am I really grinding my hips against his erection? And I don't stop. Although I should. There are hundreds of reasons why I should stop.

This is highly unprofessional. Like, not a little bit wrong, but a major, hard stop, 'Do not pass go' kind of wrong. Not that we work together. It isn't like I'm his boss, or he's mine, but this isn't the time or place for hormones to take over.

Just a little more friction.

I grind against him and dig my fingers into the back of his neck, pulling him down, or trying to claw my way up his towering height.

What am I thinking? Or doing?

Wow, but he tastes amazing. It's that kind of sinful, sultry, dark, give-me-more kind of taste I can't get enough of.

Third, this isn't—I'm not that kind of girl. Hot and heavy are never words used to describe anything sexual about my existence. The quiet, reserved, shy one, I haven't had a boyfriend in years, with the horrible exception of the asshole, Rick. And I've never experienced unbridled passion.

In contrast to the bumbling attempts Rick made, this nameless man tastes like sin and moves with unapologetic determination in his quest for more.

What the hell did he say his name was?

Not to mention, we just met, but there's no denying what I want at the hands of this man. There's simply something about him I can't explain.

I'm not the girl who kisses on the first date. None of this stops my hands from exploring the hard planes of his chest or tracing the rippled terrace of muscles spanning his back. My hands move with a mind of their own, wandering, exploring, memorizing every sculpted nuance of muscle girding his frame.

The excuse I give my mother about not dating is always the same. There's never time. All my potentials are arrogant assholes. The men I work with aren't the kind I date. Don't shit where you eat. There's great wisdom to that saying. And when not working, my life is that of a hermit: isolated, alone, and safe from the eventual heartbreak men bring.

In the end, they're all arrogant assholes who care about nothing except their next lay, and I'll be damned if I let a man use me and toss me aside the next morning.

Am I doing that now?

Who the hell cares?

This, this explosion of passion might be worth the risk.

I tilt my head back as his fingers stroke my hair. The gentle glide feels amazing but isn't nearly as mind-blowing as when he tugs at the roots. That makes my insides churn and my lady-bits pulse with aching need. It does things inside my head as well; dark, delicious, and forbidden things.

I wrap my arms around his waist and try really hard not to wrap my leg around his and climb on board. Ruggedly handsome, blue eyes, authoritative.

Check, check, and double—no, triple-check.

He's everything I can't resist in one dominating package. I'm one step away from dry humping him right here.

Men don't look at me the way he does, all hungry and determined. I've read about such things, but never experienced it. And my body? What is with all the tingly nerves?

That warmth that spreads outward from my heart? And the needy pulsations between my legs? Rubbing against his very hard erection is something I have to consciously choose not to do. I'm not a needy and weak thing who loses my mind the moment a man kisses me, current situation being a notable exception to that rule.

But damn, what a kiss.

The acceleration of my heart intensifies as he sweeps his tongue along the seam of my mouth. My hands grip the fabric of his shirt as his fingers tighten and yank on my hair. Why does that seem to be the one thing that drives me the most insane?

I know the answer to that, even if I don't want to admit it. There's a reason I don't date. Men are intimidated by what I do for a living. Put off by my hardness and strength, none ever step up to the plate to take control.

This guy doesn't seem to have a problem with taking charge, and my entire body takes notice. I crave more, even if I will never, ever voice my true desires. Forbidden, those remain relegated to the darkness of my late-night dreams. Besides, what will he do if I say something and he thinks it's weird?

Goosebumps line my skin, and it isn't because I'm cold. My

flight suit might have soaked me to the bone, but electricity skates along my skin and tunnels along my nerves. I may have been cold a few minutes ago, but a fire burns within me now.

So hot!

I want to strip out of my clothes and rub against every inch of his skin.

His shirt needs to come off.

I pull at the fabric. Grasping, I yank his shirt from where it's tucked in his pants. I have every intention of pulling it over his head and stripping him bare when he ends the kiss.

"Luv, if you do that, there is only one way this is going to end."

He presses his forehead against mine and those piercing blue eyes of his sear my soul. Warmth envelopes my wrists as he grips my hands. I give a whimper as he tugs.

"As much as I'd love to strip you out of your clothes and bury myself deep inside of you, there are men back there who might be wondering what's taking us so long. I'm sure your crew is eager to know if they're prepping for a flight or hunkering down for the next forty-eight hours as this thing blows over."

I relinquish my hold and allow him to lift my hands to his mouth. His lips press against my knuckles as he gives each a kiss.

"Fuck," he says with a growl, "but you taste like sin."

With the power of the kiss fading, a sense of shyness and uncertainty overcomes me. Is this regret? Do I feel bad about that kiss? My brows scrunch together as conflicting emotions rush through my mind.

"Hey," he says, "penny for your thoughts? Don't shut me out. After a kiss like that, you can be damn sure I'm barely getting started. I don't like the way your brows are pinching together. Do you regret what just happened?"

"No." My hands lift, and my fingers feel the puffiness of my lips. "What's happening?"

"Something amazing." He draws back, stooping to look me in the eyes. "Definitely something amazing, and that's just a warmup."

"What does that mean?"

Raw desire fills his words. "It means I want to know if your pussy tastes as good as your lips, and how it's going to feel when I slam my cock in real deep. I'm not a slow as you go kind of guy, Ariel." He gives a smirk. "At least, not once things get started. When we fuck, you can be damn certain you'll never forget me. Is that what you want?"

Actually, it isn't what I want at all. A quick and hasty fuck? It might feel good in the heat of the moment. If he fucks with any of the devastation of his kisses, it might be worth it, but I will regret it every day for the rest of my life. My heart isn't wired for a one-and-done fling. As silly as it sounds, I believe in true love, romance, and finding the one I want.

"About that …" I can barely look at him.

"Shush," he says.

"It's just, I don't think——"

"If the next words out of your mouth are that you don't think we should've done that, then you and I are going to have a problem. I don't regret that kiss, and I damn well plan on doing it again."

"Why's that?" I have every right to say no, even if that's not what I want at all.

"You and I are going to finish this. My balls are going to ache like hell until I can slip deep inside you, but we've got shit to deal with first. Like the others."

A shiver races down my spine, making me jump. The residual heat of that kiss still burns in my blood. My entire body aches. Maybe not in the way he says. Women don't suffer blue balls and all, but—I rub my thighs together—I ache.

Then his words finally make it through the haze of lust shrouding my mind.

The others.

"Oh shit." My eyes widen.

How long have we been away? Andrew and Larry have a good idea of how long it should take to check the weather. If they ever find out what I did with this guy, I'll never hear the end of it. Not to mention my reputation will be shot.

The worst thing a woman in my field can do is sleep around,

and here I've been practically dry humping the leg of a man I just met. That's all they'll see.

"Um … we need to get back." I roll my lower lip and bite at it.

"Yes, luv, we do, but don't think for a minute we're not finishing this."

"We'll see."

His eyes narrow as he stares me down. "I don't think you're understanding me here." He gestures between us. "This is far from over."

"Consider it a one-time thing. Besides, I don't even know your name."

He tilts his head back and lets out the deepest laugh. "You've got to be fucking kidding me. I had my tongue down your throat and you don't remember my name? I think I'm offended."

"I was a little distracted."

His eyes glint with mischief and he pulls me tight to his side. "I can accept that, but not the rest. Although I see it in your eyes. Go ahead and try to run away. I enjoy the chase."

He leans down and plants another devastating kiss on my lips. My nerves light up and my stomach tumbles about.

I'm flying.

No, I'm falling.

The entire room spins and tilts beneath my feet. My hand against his chest does nothing to settle all the spinning and dropping and floating, and boy does he taste good. The slow beat of his heart pulses beneath the palm of my hand. An island of calm amid the chaos of that kiss, do I have the same effect on him as he had on me?

"My name is Aiden Cole, and it has been my pleasure making your acquaintance." He pulls back and gazes down at me.

I try to steady myself on my feet. He holds me by the waist until my wobbling stops.

"There's something you need to know about me," he says.

Still trying to regain my composure, I rock back and avoid looking at him. If I do that, I'll fall under the spell of his amazing eyes.

"What's that?" I gather my hair at my nape and quickly reform it into a bun, securing it into place on the back of my head. Anything to keep me distracted from his next words.

"I'm a take-charge kind of guy."

"Is that so?" He gives a nod and I shake my head. "I think we need to head back and give everyone the bad news."

"After you, ladies first."

He wiggles his eyebrows, and the subtext isn't lost on me. It's going to be a long couple of days.

Chapter Six

Aiden

THE FEMALE PILOT PUTS MY ENTIRE BODY ON HIGH ALERT. HARD AS A rock, I reach down to adjust my frustration, a feat made worse with the knowledge it'll be days before I can quench my thirst.

It's going to be one hell of a rough ride, both the storm and chasing Ariel. Something happened and I don't understand the switch that flicked in her head.

Puzzles intrigue me, however, and I determine I'll get to the bottom of this one. Hot and heavy one instant—she practically climbed on top of me during that kiss—then a cooling off that ventured toward near frigid?

It doesn't make sense.

That doesn't bother me. The best things are worthy of determined pursuit, and I have a feeling this is a woman who warrants a chase. This is going to be fun, and already the gears in my mind churn with all the ways I can torment her until she has no choice but to surrender.

Determined to peel back all of her layers, I'll get in her head and dig in so deep it'll be impossible for her not to think about me.

That's all I need to win her over. Get her to where she can't stop thinking about me, and the battle is all but won.

I give a chuckle as she stiffens her spine, fists her hands, and tries to storm out. A violent shiver stops her in her tracks, reminding me to make a detour.

Hell, if I bring her back to my quarters, we'll never leave.

Sensitive to the difficulties women in my world face when it comes to earning hard-won respect and keeping it, I won't jeopardize what she's worked to build by taking her to my room for a quick fuck.

Maybe a detour isn't the best option.

I'll take her back to the others and then get her something to change into, preferably something of mine. The thought of her wearing my clothes makes my dick twitch.

When she reaches the sickbay, I hold the door open while she slips inside.

"It's a no-go for the flight," I announce to my crew.

Ariel's men glance up and look to her for confirmation. I appreciate their loyalty, and it speaks much to what they think of her.

"Winds are too high to take off," she explains. "Aiden assures me we can wait out the storm here."

"Is it safe?" Andrew turns to me. "Why evacuate when you could've kept everyone here. Seems expensive to offload an entire crew."

"Right now, staying is safer than trying to fly ahead of a hurricane. As for standard procedures, it's safer to ride out a storm on land than on the rig. We can repair equipment," I gesture to my two wounded crew, "but people are our greatest investment and their safety our highest priority. I'm not going to lie. It's not going to be a picnic, and we're in for a rough ride, but the rig hasn't sunk yet. Sorry guys."

"Well, shit," Larry says.

"What about them," Ariel goes to Jeffery and examines the splints we placed. "Can they wait?"

"Thought you said we didn't have a choice," Andrew replies.

"We don't," she answers.

"Well, it would be best if we can get them to a hospital, but they're not critical. It's going to be rough. Jeffery's legs are broken, but the pulses are good in his feet. I don't think there's any internal bleeding. Without x-rays, there's no telling. We'll just have to keep a close eye on him. I can try to keep him as comfortable as possible."

"And the other?" she asks. "What's his name?"

The way she focuses on my injured crewmen increases my growing respect for the pilot. Her compassion makes her sexier, if that's possible.

"Caleb has a concussion," Andrew answers. "There's no way to know if there's anything more serious going on in his head. I'm most concerned about him, but we were able to get him to wake and follow commands. He's not going to like us at the end of this."

"Why's that?" I ask, curious about the comment.

"We need to wake him every hour. Although, there's nothing we can do if he doesn't rouse. We'll just have to hope for the best." Andrew glances around the sickbay. "Do you mind if I have a look around?"

"Our sickbay is modestly equipped, but whatever you need is yours. Sadly, there aren't any x-ray machines, but we do have the ability to call back to shore if you want to check in with our doc remotely."

"I think that's a great idea," Ariel chimes in. "Maybe you can call their doc while I call our transport coordinator and give them an update."

"On it." Andrew turns to Larry. "Why don't you poke around and see what you can find? Y'all have a pharmacy on board?"

"We do," I say. "Not sure what all is there, basic stuff I'm sure. Antibiotics and painkillers mostly."

"Well, that sounds perfect." Andrew stands and presses his hands on his thighs. "Where's this phone?"

I have my men help Ariel's crew. With the evacuation, most station personnel left their belongings behind, which might help to find them dry clothes to wear. I gesture to Duncan. "Hey, come with me."

"Sure thing, boss," Duncan says. "What's up?"

"Since our guests will be staying, let's scrounge them up some dry clothes, and we should probably take stock of the galley and figure out food."

Duncan smirks. "Ever ridden out a storm on one of these?"

"Once."

"And?"

"It's not something I look forward to repeating."

"How about that pilot? She might make things easier," he says.

"If you lay a hand on her, it'll be the last thing you do." I give a low warning growl.

"Hey, that's not what I meant." He points to the ring on his finger. "I got a sexy as fuck wife with a kid on the way. I was talking about you. It's about time you break your dry spell."

"What?"

"Well, it just seemed y'all were gone for a bit, and from the way she's most definitely not looking at you, I was just wondering."

"Don't. There's nothing going on that concerns you." It isn't a complete lie but skirts the truth by a wide margin. "Speaking of, let's figure out quarters. I want everyone to stay close."

"I can handle that. So, quarters and food. Anything else?"

"Who's about the same size as Andrew and Larry? We need to find them something dry to wear and should probably wash what they have."

"Great, getting ready to ride out a storm and you have me on laundry detail."

I laugh. "I know, we're living the high life. Now, who in the crew is closest to the pilot in size?"

Women are rare on oil rigs. Unfortunately, our rig doesn't have any female crew.

Duncan scrunches up his face. "I think there's one or two."

"Okay, you do that. Find her some pants. I'll grab her a shirt and sweatshirt. She's shivering and nearly hypothermic, although I don't think she'll let that stop her. Change of clothes for them all, food, then quarters."

"Gotcha, boss," Duncan says with another smirk. "On it."

I separate from Duncan and head to my quarters. While living conditions on the rigs are austere, improvements to crew facilities over the years make things more livable. Personnel live in modular living facilities. Depending on position, we bunk two or four to a room. I'm one of the few who enjoys a private room.

I head there now, needing a moment to relieve the pent-up energy inside me. Ariel and her men are safe inside the sickbay with Randall there to help them with anything they need. This gives me a moment to unwind, call my bosses, and take care of a very pressing need.

After I inform my supervisors we'll be forced to wait out the storm on the rig, I dial my mother-in-law.

"Aiden!" Her bright eyes stare out of the screen at me. A lot of people think oil rigs are remote, but we have high-speed satellite internet, which means I keep in touch with my daughter nearly every day. "When are you getting home? Hurricane Julian has picked up speed. They say it's going to be a direct hit."

"Is Callie still awake?"

"I just put her down. She wanted to wait up until her daddy got home."

"About that …" I explain the injuries to my crewmen while readying the rig for the storm, the arrival of the medevac crew, and how Ariel made the call, grounding the helicopter. "So, we're not going to be able to fly out. Do you have everything you need?"

"Yes, of course. I keep everything on your list just in case. We're official preppers! Bring on the apocalypse." She raises her fist in mock salute.

"Mary …"

"Hey, you're the one with the lists and the storage closets filled to the brim with everything and anything we might need. And before you ask, I've already cleaned and plugged the bathtubs. They're filling up as we speak."

"Look, I'm sorry I won't be there to ride out the storm with you and Callie."

"Aiden, this isn't my first hurricane, and this is nothing like the super typhoons Richard and I endured in Okinawa. We'll be fine.

Two girls partying it out. If we're lucky we'll lose power and will have to light the candles. Callie made me put one by her bed … just in case. Don't worry about us."

Samantha's mother is a rare jewel. I count myself lucky I married into her family. Mary welcomed me like a son. She's tough as nails. Wife of a Marine, she spent most of her marriage raising two daughters alone and often overseas while her husband was deployed.

Nothing scares Mary, and she passed those traits on to her daughter and her granddaughter. Callie has the best role model in the world to raise her, a fearless woman who embraces everything life has to offer, even when faced with tragedy.

"Well, I wanted to blow Callie a kiss."

"I can take you to her if you want."

"You said she's asleep?"

I really want to see my daughter's shining blue eyes and mop of blonde curls. It hurts to be separated from her, especially with a storm on the way.

I'm not worried about Mary and Callie. They live far enough inland that they should only see the outer wind bands and heavy rains. Nevertheless, it'll be hard not being with them.

"She's dead asleep, but I can wake her. It's been a busy day prepping for the storm."

"Don't wake her, but tiptoe in. I want to see my baby doll."

Mary brings the phone into Callie's room and holds it where I can see my daughter sleeping. She's curled up in bed, snuggled beneath a camo-pink comforter. That bedspread embraces her tomboy, rough and tough attitude, as well as her love for all things pink. I blow her a silent kiss.

"Sweet dreams," I say in a whisper.

I can worry about my daughter, but there's no need. Callie has the best protector on the planet in a grandmother who isn't afraid of anything. I hope Callie grows up with the same take-charge attitude.

The screen shifts and I stare at the floor while Mary walks me back into the kitchen. She props the phone on the counter and folds her arms across her chest.

"So, tell me about this pilot."

"What about the pilot?"

"Oh, Aiden, you think I was born yesterday? The helicopter pilot? The only one you mentioned by name."

"I didn't—"

"Son, first off, I know the sound a man makes when a woman has caught his eye."

"But—"

She holds up her finger, shushing me. "Second, you don't have to feel guilty about being attracted to another woman. Samantha doesn't want you to waste your life pining away for her. It's okay to be interested …"

"I never said—"

"I'm not saying this Ariel is the one you want, but I am saying it's been far too long since you took a chance on any woman. You're stuck out in the middle of the Gulf, getting ready to face down a beast of a storm, you really should loosen up a bit and see what happens. You might lose power there too and need to snuggle—"

"Mary!"

She snickers. "Oh, you know what I mean."

I know exactly what she means.

I clear my throat. "I'm a little uncomfortable talking about this with my mother-in-law …"

"Fine, we won't talk about it, but you made a promise to Sam. It's okay to fall in love again, and you aren't being unfaithful to your dead wife if you do."

"Mary, that's a low blow."

"Look, Sam was the light of my life. No mother should have to bury her daughter. But I did. Now, I celebrate her life and honor her memory. She wanted you to find someone to love. It's what I did when I lost Richard. I'm out there, playing the field. Just the other day …"

I sit down while Mary tells me about her latest beau, happy that the subject of Ariel disappears beneath my mother-in-law's overly descriptive, oversharing of a very active love life. After another ten minutes, I say my goodbyes.

A quick search through my drawers and I find a T-shirt and pair of sweats Ariel can use, at least until after we do her laundry. The thought of her completely naked and wrapped in my clothes makes me painfully hard again.

Chapter Seven

Ariel

I DO WHAT I CAN TO HELP LARRY SEARCH THE SMALL SICKBAY. THERE are a lot of bandages we don't need. *Jackpot!* I grab a couple of bags filled with fluid and bring them over to Andrew.

"Will this help?"

"Lactated Ringers?" He examines the bag of IV fluid, checking the expiration date. "This is perfect." The man beside him groans. "Now, if we can find some pain killers. All I have is morphine, and that's not the best for them."

"Why not? Won't it get rid of their pain?" It seems more humane to knock both men out and let the storm pass over while they're out of it.

"Yes, but it depresses breathing. I need them as alert as possible."

Randall speaks up. "We have a limited pharmacy. Might be something there, although it's locked up."

"How much trouble will we get into if we break that lock?" I ask.

Andrew stretches, leaning back, then he twists side to side. "I'm thinking we'll be forgiven. Where is it?"

Aiden returns. The way he fills the doorway makes my breath hitch and my pulse pound. Our kiss plays on endless repeat in my mind since he left the room. It's all I can do to focus on searching the small sickbay.

He cocks his head, taking me in as he casually leans against the doorjamb. He changed out of his rain gear into jeans and a T-shirt.

Well-worn denim drapes low over his hips, cups his groin, and fills with the muscular bulk of his thighs. I shouldn't stare, especially at the impressive bulge behind that zipper, but find it difficult to shift my attention anywhere else.

If anyone notices, I'll be mortified, but Andrew, Larry, and Randall are busy searching the small room behind me. Duncan has yet to return. Our two patients are in no condition to pay attention to anyone.

But Aiden?

Once I tear my gaze away from his crotch, the heat of his smoldering gaze tells me he didn't miss a thing. He reaches down and adjusts himself while I watch. I gulp and try to turn around, but his deep, rumbly voice demands attention.

"I brought a shirt and sweatpants for you to change into. Duncan is looking around to see what we can scavenge for your team. We should get you out of those clothes." A wink follows, telling me he's more than happy to assist in that task.

"Um, thank you."

I cast a glance toward the others, but none of the men pay any attention to me or Aiden. He knows it too and licks his lips.

He hands me the clothes and lowers his voice to a whisper. "I'd rather be taking clothes off you than putting them on. But if you're going to wear anything, it'll be something of mine." He gives me a hard look. "If you try to argue with me about this, you're going to lose."

"Aiden ..."

He shakes his head. "We're not even close to being done."

The echo of his words from earlier sends my heart into a dizzying spin.

He continues, keeping his tone conversational in case the others listen in. "Now, we have laundry facilities here, of course, and can get your clothes washed. Until then, you can wear these."

"Bossy much?" I say under my breath.

"That depends on whether you like it or not, but I already know the answer to that."

I arch a brow, waiting for him to continue, but he pushes his clothes into my hands and steps away. His crewman, Duncan, returns with an armful of jeans and shirts.

"Hey, found some stuff for you guys," Duncan calls out to my men.

I retreat to the sickbay, placing distance between myself and Aiden. It doesn't work. Aiden follows, staying right beside me. A respectful distance separates us.

No one knows about the electricity sizzling between us, but I feel every blazing lick of the heat from his gaze. An inferno stirs to life between us, and I need to find a way to put out the blaze.

As the pilot, I'm technically in command of our mission. We aren't a military unit but adhere to many of the same conventions when it comes to the chain of command. With the helicopter grounded for the foreseeable future, I have nothing to contribute to the care of the wounded men, but I can do the laundry. As much as it grates on me to volunteer for such a mundane job, there is no one else.

"If you guys change, I'll do the wash." I inject false cheer into my voice.

Talking about the laundry keeps me from thinking about the man standing far too close. That side of my body heats being so near to him.

Aiden takes a step back, gives me an odd look, then a respectful nod. "I can help with that."

"Oh, no need." I don't need his help. That means more alone time with him, and I won't survive another second of that.

"It's the least I can do," he insists with a wink.

Can he read my mind?

"Randall, you stay and help these guys out. Maybe we can get

Jeffery and Caleb better situated. Duncan, you're on galley duty. Ariel and I will come up with shift assignments."

He turns to me, taking the time to include me in his plans, even as he makes them without my consultation.

"I'm thinking we split up your guys and pair them with mine. We all have basic first aid training, so we can help out as you need. Duncan, why don't you and Andrew pair up. Randall, you and Larry are a team. I'll take the pilot. We'll set a twelve-hour shift schedule. I'll leave it to you to figure out who takes the first shift."

"Sounds like a plan," Duncan says.

"Good," Aiden continues. "I'll show Ariel to my quarters so she can change, but if y'all want to strip out of your clothes and leave them in a pile here, we'll be back for a laundry run. We need to orient each of you to the rig. My only rule during this whole thing is no one wanders around alone, and no one goes outside. You've all got your buddy assignments." He sweeps his arm out and gestures toward the door. "Ariel? After you."

I need to find my voice, but that is impossible with the lump in my throat. He orchestrates the perfect plan to maximize his time alone with me. I'm not sure if that pisses me off or turns me on.

Gulping, I turn to my men. "Is there anything you need?"

Andrew shakes his head. "The IV bags are a godsend, and we found analgesics in the pharmacy. You said quarters?" He turns his attention to Aiden. "Any chance they're more comfortable than the gurneys in here?"

"Minimally." Aiden crosses his arms.

Andrew gives a nod. "I think it would be best if we transported them out of here, but I'd like to see what we're talking about."

"Duncan can show you where you'll be bunking, but I think it's best for Jeffery and Caleb if they stay here."

"Gotcha." Andrew focuses his next words on me. "You okay?"

I don't miss the protective undertones. From the way Aiden stiffens beside me, he doesn't either.

"Yeah, I'm just going to change, and I'll be right back."

Andrew gives me a grin and a slight incline of his head. "This is not how I thought this day would go."

"I know, right?"

With those words, I enter the hall, leaving behind the protection of the group to face Aiden alone. An awakening pulses between my legs as the memory of that kiss takes center stage in my mind.

"This way." The timbre of Aiden's voice turns low and gravelly, raspy with suppressed need.

I understand that well. My skin feels hot. My heart rate speeds up. My stomach flips around in my belly. Not one step out into the hall, and I'm a trembling heap of hormones, replete with weak knees, racing heart, and nerves surging with overstimulation.

We didn't do anything more than kiss, and yet lingering adrenaline spikes in my body with the thought of once again being alone with him. Despite all the promises I made to myself, I can't ignore what my body wants.

The raw desire darkening Aiden's features tells me the feeling is mutual. Desperation claws at me and I battle my emotions using reason to fight the overwhelming urges swirling inside of my body.

I grip the damp fabric of my flight suit, wanting Aiden to ease my torment. Fear has me firmly in its grip, along with its cousin desire. These feelings aren't something I've ever experienced before.

Coming unglued with a man isn't what I do.

One part of me wishes for Aiden to soothe my fears and make all the tormented thoughts disappear, but another part wishes for him to let me fall. If only so he can catch me.

When we turn the corner, leaving the open door of the sickbay behind us, I expect him to spin me around until my back hits the wall and kiss me again. Instead, he shoulders past me and leads me down a long hallway. With a tight grip on my flight suit, I take in a deep breath and follow.

He makes two turns and then stops by a closed door. Everything around us has an industrial feel, taste, and smell to it. All hard edges, steel forms nearly every surface. From the plating of the floor beneath my boots to the cold, unyielding walls, nothing speaks of warmth and comfort. Even the door is heavy steel. He turns the doorknob and swings the door inward.

"Your accommodations for the next ... however long." He

braces the door, placing his hand high over my head, forcing me to duck beneath the flex of his biceps.

"Thank you."

As I step beneath him, he gives a deep groan. "Ariel?"

"Yes?"

"You're addictive."

"Excuse me?"

"And you smell incredible." He inhales deeply.

"I'm sure I smell like oil, grease, and sweat."

"And you don't think I find that intoxicating?"

"I—I don't know what to say to that." The power of his gaze destroys any resolve I have left.

If he leans down …

If he wraps an arm around my waist …

If he took my hair in his fist again …

"Say yes," he rasps.

"To what?" I don't know what he's asking. There are too many things hanging in the balance.

"That you feel it too. Tell me I'm not insane."

"Aiden, I don't know—"

Without another word, he pushes me into the room. The door slams shut, and he spins me around until my back does, in fact, hit the wall. He reaches behind my head and tugs on the bun, freeing it from its restraints. With his hand gripping my hair, he lowers his mouth until it hovers over mine, a kiss away.

"The air crackles between us, igniting something I haven't felt in a very long time. I don't know you, but I feel as if I do. It's painful to be in the same room with you and not be able to touch you, to kiss you, to taste you, and take you like I need."

His words whisper through me, licking my nerve endings with sparks of arousal, which fizz, and pop, and crackle until my entire body comes alive and buzzes with a restless energy.

Yeah, I feel it too.

My heart swoons. It dips. It soars. And I cringe.

My emotions are all over the place. A few minutes ago, I was determined to stay as far away from him as possible. That one kiss would have been our first and last. Professionalism demands I keep my distance, but his seductive words speak to a truth I feel deep inside.

I don't know how to respond, so I say nothing and hold perfectly still. Breathing is nearly impossible with his towering presence looming over me. My gaze darts between his lips and his penetrating stare. The power and ferocity behind that look turns my legs to jelly and liquefies me from the inside out. I want everything he offers.

His bulk makes me feel small, feminine, and soft. Emotions and feelings I'm not used to. Clearly, he works out, whether from the demands of the job or from dedicated time in the gym, he has the kind of body women drool over. Fortunately, there aren't any other women present, which means no competition.

I never win those.

His muscles flex with agitation as he barely holds on to his restraint. Bulging biceps, shoulders brimming with power, pectorals which fill out the cotton of the T-shirt and strain to cover his chest. I already felt the ridges and valleys of the sharply honed muscles beneath that shirt and ache to explore it all once again.

While his lips hang a breath away from mine, I lift a hand to his chest, awestruck by his power and virility. Is it possible that he can be mine? That he wants me?

No competition…

That thought keeps swirling in my head, but another more insidious one rises to take its place. I might be nothing more than another notch on his bedpost, something to pass the time while we're stuck out in the middle of the Gulf. But what if what he says is true, and he wants more? After a string of failed relationships, is it possible a man truly wants me?

He stares down at me with the arrogance of a man who knows he's won. His lids lower to a dark and sultry half-mast while a devilish grin stretches across his face.

"You're thinking about having sex with me," he says in triumph.

Arrogance aside, I don't immediately respond. Desire hums in my veins, riding the high of hormones given permission to run wild.

I can do this. Right?

I'm often teased as being *high-strung*, but what will it feel like to let loose? Can I take a chance and see where things might go?

"Not as much as you're thinking about it."

I refuse to cave in and become a forgettable fuck. Letting go, it seems, is harder than simply thinking it.

"Damn straight, I'm thinking about it. I haven't stopped, and just so you know, I've already fucked you against this wall, on that desk, in that bed, and taken you from behind while you're on all fours. I've had you kneeling at my feet with my cock sliding in and out of your mouth, and I'm thinking about taking you against the wall again."

"I'm amazed at the stamina that requires. You sure you have that in you?" My nipples peak with the desire for him to do exactly that. "There are four men back there who think I've come here to change out of my clothes. To do everything you say takes a lot more time than changing my shirt unless I'm wrong about your stamina."

He tilts his head back and roars with a deep belly laugh. "Shit, woman, talk like that will get you tossed over my knee."

That image has me squeezing my thighs together, but that only makes the burning ache worse.

His mouth floats over my lips. Suddenly the room seems too small. I clutch at his shirt, pushing him away while simultaneously pulling him toward me.

He still hasn't kissed me, but he's near enough to feel the zing of fleeting contact. Sparks indeed. The entire room buzzes with the energy sizzling between us.

"I'm going to kiss you," he pronounces, "and I don't know if I'll be able to stop."

My fingers twist in the fabric of his shirt, sending all the wrong signals and yet saying exactly what I feel. I part my lips and that tiny movement is enough to close the space between us. An electrical charge zaps at my lips and races along my nerves, sending a shock wave rippling across my skin. I don't move. I don't dare.

He doesn't either, letting the moment stretch between us, a moment suspended in time while he gives me a choice. This is the time to say no. He stares at me, eyes darkening with lust.

I stare right back and face the raw, carnal desire brimming in his eyes. This is what attraction feels like. It's nothing I've ever experienced before, and hell if I can resist it. My entire body buzzes with adrenaline and burns with an aching fire.

"Aiden ..." I stretch up on tiptoe and thread my fingers together behind his neck.

With a deep growl, he presses me against the wall, lifting me up as he claims that kiss. My legs wrap around his hips. My body acts on instinct, no longer with me in control.

He seizes my mouth with bruising aggression. There is nothing tender in the kiss. He claims, and I surrender. His tongue sweeps along the seam of my lips, then dives in to chase mine. Firm and determined, his lips press against mine, demanding nothing but complete and absolute submission. I give that to him, knowing this will set the tone for everything that follows.

This isn't our first kiss. It lacks the nervousness and cautious exploration while sharing the same reckless hunger. I follow his lead, giving him complete control over what happens next.

My tongue follows his, my lips surrender, my thighs clench around his hips as his grip tightens around my waist. He lifts one hand and runs his fingers through my hair. Gripping tight, he forces my head to slant as he desires. He rocks against me, pressing into the space between my legs.

His mouth glides over mine, tongue licking, teasing, taking, and I drown beneath the onslaught. My hips grind against him as I slowly lose control of any restraint I have left.

He yanks my hair, causing me to cry out as he deepens the kiss, turning it into something raw and wild. One hand threads in my hair; he uses the other to palm my ass. Those fingers continue their exploration, following the seam of my flight suit until they brush against my sex.

If not for my clothes, I have no doubt he would shove his fingers deep inside.

I still the movement of my hips, slowing the grind I can barely control. We either need to stop ... or strip.

Chapter Eight

Aiden

MY ENTIRE BODY ACHES. I'M TRYING TO SHOVE MY DICK INTO ARIEL, but too much clothing stands in my way. My body has only one task on its mind, while I consider the repercussions.

I really shouldn't be thinking right now.

This has the mark of a bad idea written all over it. Not that I can help myself. Ariel is imminently fuckable, but the others are waiting for our return. If they don't suspect some degree of attraction between me and the pilot, they most certainly will if I return her looking freshly fucked.

My hips surge forward again, desperate for more contact, more friction, more heat.

Damn, but I want this woman with a hunger I've never felt before. Not even with Samantha, not that I'm comparing the two.

But dammit! This can't be right. I feel it, though, a ravenous need raging inside of me.

I slip my tongue deep in Ariel's mouth, needing a final taste, and then I do the unthinkable. With a nip to her lip, I end the kiss, pulling back with regret.

My dick aches with unspent need and roars for completion, but I don't want to take Ariel like this. When I do take her, I want to savor the entire experience.

"Fuck, Ariel, but …"

"Aiden?" Her stormy eyes look at me and glaze over with lust.

"We gotta get you out of these clothes." I hold back a groan because that's exactly what I want; Ariel naked and wrapped around me as I sink into her wet heat.

I disentangle her legs from around my hips and wait until she is steady on her feet. Once she stands without assistance, I take a step back and stab my fingers into my hair, jerking at the roots.

The pain helps me focus on what I should do rather than what I want to do. I take another step, and then another until I come up against the opposite wall. These prefabricated living quarters come with a premium on space.

I wish I could put more distance between us because all I want is to unzip my fly, strip her out of her clothes, and finish what we began. But, it's my responsibility to take care of her, and that means not letting her make the biggest mistake of her life.

Her reputation isn't worth a quick fuck. Not to mention I don't want to ruin what we have before we even begin. There's more to Ariel than a one-night stand. She smells like my forever.

"I want you." I tug at my hair and draw my elbows together in front of my face. She needs to know how much I want her, but also what I'll do to protect her. "But, we need to get back before we're missed."

I don't miss her deep breathing. How can I when her breasts heave up and down? The woman is a knockout. She might be covered in a baggy flight suit, but I have a good idea what I'll find underneath.

I point to the door. "I'm going to step out while you change."

"Aiden …" Her eyes shimmer.

"You know exactly what will happen if I don't because there's no way I'll stop. I don't want your men, or my crew, talking about what might or might not have happened in here."

She takes in a couple of deep breaths and gives a nod. "I …"

Her entire body shudders, then she looks at me and gives a weak smile. "Thank you."

"Don't thank me, hun. I have every intention of defiling you, but not at the expense of making a spectacle of it. This thing between us ... stays between us. You hear me?"

She gives a slow nod. "I do." Then she shakes her head. "I told myself I wouldn't let you kiss me, but I couldn't stop."

"I know, but you were humping me pretty damn hard." I love the flush in her face. "Don't worry, doll, I'll get you stripped for real and screaming my name before too long. For now ..." I point to the door again. "It's safer if I wait outside."

"Okay."

"And one other thing."

"Yes?"

"I want your bra and panties off under my clothes. Next time we're alone, I want to feel you."

The poor thing gulps, and that makes my heart rate spike.

I pull on the door and leave her alone to change. My cock protests, and I agree. Leaving that room may be the hardest thing I've done in years. A quick readjustment helps relieve some of the ache in my dick.

I need to rub one out, or I'm going to go insane.

Boots slap on the floor from down the hall. I slump to the floor and draw my knees to my chest. No need for anyone to see the tenting of my pants. Duncan rounds the corner and pulls up short. His gaze flicks to the door and his brows arch.

"Didn't expect to see you out here, sitting on the floor."

"Watch it," I say, sharper than intended, then cover it with a laugh. "I don't know why women always take so damned long to change."

Duncan's face splits into a grin. "Yeah, my wife takes forever, too."

I need to shift the topic of conversation. Duncan is entirely too perceptive.

"How's it going back there?"

"Not too bad. Caleb woke up for a second. The flight nurse said that was a good sign."

"How is he?"

"Caleb or the nurse?"

"Caleb."

"Disorientated. Groggy. His speech is slurred, but he knows his name, the date, and that there's a storm coming. Andrew says those are good things. He seems to be a pretty damn good flight nurse, really knows his stuff. I guess they have to keep waking him up every hour, though, with the concussion."

"How does that help?"

"I have no clue." Duncan gives a shrug.

"Did you come looking for me? Or just wandering the halls?"

"A little of both."

"What part of buddy-up did you not understand?"

"Aw, come on. You don't mean that for us."

I arch a brow. "How can I expect them to follow that rule if my own crew doesn't?"

"Well, I wasn't looking for you. I was actually heading to the galley."

"Taking the long way around?"

"Unless you want me outside. I actually do listen to you sometimes. This is the shortest way."

Ah, I forgot about that. The galley is located two levels down. From the sickbay, the quickest route is outside and down the stairs. Duncan might be wandering alone, but he's at least adhering to that rule.

"Have you looked outside recently?" I'm curious how the storm is doing.

Duncan gives me a sheepish look. "It's getting bad out there."

"You went outside, didn't you?" My eyes narrow as Duncan looks away.

"I opened the door and shut it just as quick. This thing coming at us is a beast. Have you looked at the storm track recently?" Duncan isn't scared. He loves storms and practically bounces with excitement.

"No."

I've been busy with other things, like how far I can shove my tongue down Ariel's throat. It's time to focus and prepare for Julian's arrival.

"Not that it makes one bit of difference," Duncan says, "but it's coming straight for us."

"That should be interesting," I say. "Have you ever been in the eye of a storm?"

"This will be the first time." Duncan crosses his arms and leans against the bulkhead.

Thoughts of the storm take care of my raging erection. I feel comfortable standing up. "We need to keep a close eye on this thing."

"No shit," Duncan agrees. "I was going to whip up something for dinner and see what I could prep ahead of time. If we lose power, at least we won't go hungry."

"Hungry? We're stocked to feed over a hundred hands. I don't think that's going to be a problem."

"Well, I'm more of a comfort food kind of guy. If you want to live off cold cereal, so be it. I'm cooking dinner and breakfast. Julian should pass overhead by morning, don't you think? Then we're halfway done as the trailing edge slams back into us."

"I don't know. Let's check the weather map."

The door to my room opens. "Hey, Duncan." Ariel gives Duncan a tentative wave. "What's going on?"

I jerk my thumb toward Duncan. "He's headed to the galley to cook, and we're headed to the bridge to take a look at Julian's path. Duncan says the storm shifted its path and will head right over us."

She looks between the two of us, then focuses on Duncan. "You're kidding, right?"

"Not from what I saw." Duncan shoves his hands in the pockets of his jeans. "The eye should pass right overhead."

"Wow." Her fingers flutter over her belly.

I love that she doesn't ask if we'll be safe. It doesn't matter. We can't leave. Whatever happens, will happen, but this isn't the first storm the rig's endured. I have faith and realize Ariel leans on me for that support.

"It's going to be fine." There's no reason not to reassure her. "You ready to check in on Julian?"

Her tight nod makes my gut clench. Despite her calm exterior, she's scared.

Duncan steps into the gap. "Don't worry. We're going to be fine. It may get loud, and the rig will groan, but that's just her speaking to the storm. If you want, you can join me in the galley. Sometimes, keeping your hands busy helps."

She takes in a deep breath, and I think for a moment she'll go with Duncan, but then her attention shifts to me.

"That sounds great, but I need to call back to base and check in. Maybe Aiden can take me down after we're done, and we can whip something up together."

"Sounds like a plan," Duncan says. "I'll see you guys later."

"Hang on." Her attention turns to me. "Almost forgot my stuff." Ducking back inside, she returns with an armful of wet clothes.

I love the way my clothes swallow her slim frame and silence the growl of possession in my throat, knowing she wears nothing underneath them. Duncan can't leave fast enough, although, can I trust myself enough to be alone with her?

As Duncan disappears down the hall, she glances up at me through the dark fringe of her lashes. "I guess we should go check on the storm?"

"You're going to be the death of me, you know this, right?"

She nibbles at her lower lip and smiles. "Is this crazy? Has this ever happened to you before?"

Uncertainty pools in the depths of her eyes. There's more to that question than she's asking.

"If you're wondering if I'm the kind of guy who runs around kissing women he just met, let me remind you that I work on an oil rig, two weeks on, two weeks off. My time off is spent with the most adorable nine-year-old you'll ever meet. I don't have time to screw around. So, no, this doesn't happen to me. What about you?"

She practically spits out her laugh. "You're kidding, right?" She makes some vague gesture down her body, oblivious to her natural beauty. "Who would want this?"

I gape, then close my mouth. "You have no idea, do you?" Her blank stare tells me everything I need to know. I'll tell her later, but for now, we have a job to do.

"We need to get back to the others and then call in with a status update. At some point, we're going to lose communications over the satellite radio."

Her amazing lips twist as she nibbles at them. "I'm a little scared, to be honest, and I've been in some hairy situations before."

"Tell me about them."

Her head slants to the side and she regards me for a long moment. "It's not that interesting."

"Come on, female helicopter pilot, ex-military? You can't tell me there's not a story in there."

"Well actually …"

The way her eyes light up with a flood of memories makes my heart swell with an uncharacteristic warmth. Physical attraction aside, I want to climb inside this amazing woman's head to see what makes her tick. She might be scared about being stranded on an oil rig while a hurricane blows overhead, but she has the balls to tackle a male-dominated field and excel.

I'm thrilled to have her undivided attention. She speaks animatedly about her decision to go into the military and about the difficulties she faced in basic training. While we load her team's clothes into the laundry, she tells me about her selection to become a rotary wing pilot.

Chapter Nine

Ariel

TALKING ABOUT MY TIME IN THE MILITARY BRINGS A RUSH OF emotions, some good, some bad. Aiden seems interested and asks really good questions. He makes it easy to talk about everything.

I can't believe all the things I share.

"You're pretty incredible, you know." Aiden closes the door to the washing machine and fills up the detergent dispenser.

"Not really."

"Tell me about your solo flight in a helicopter. That had to be incredible."

I glance up at the ceiling and smile. It was more than incredible.

"Well, I remember setting my alarm for 8 a.m. It was a Sunday in May, and I was nervous as shit. I woke ten minutes before my alarm. Sunshine filtered through my windows and I stared at the dust dancing in the sunbeams. It was a surreal moment. I also remember being terrified and pulling the covers over my head."

"You're kidding? I can't imagine you being scared of anything."

"Well, I was. It was my first solo flight and a major step towards becoming a helicopter pilot." The same rush of emotions and adrenaline spike in my veins telling the story as when I flew my solo.

"I take it you found your way out from under the covers?"

"I did. Once I got over that little bit of fear, I jumped out, put on my uniform, and drove to the flight line. I can still feel the butterflies." I laugh. "Isn't that funny? After all these years, I can feel the jangle of my nerves. It was bad, too. I was so sick to my stomach. All my classmates were there to watch; some of them wanted to see me fail."

"Really?"

"Yeah, sad to say. They wanted to see the chick fail. I was the first in our class to solo. Many of them resented me for that." I peek up at him. "Don't ever repeat this, but I was so nervous that I puked in a trashcan right outside the training building."

"You threw up?" He slaps his hand on his thigh. "Now that, I don't believe."

"Of course, I couldn't let any of them know, but I spewed chunks. It actually made me feel ten times better, getting that out of the way."

"I guess it did. Keep going. Your story about puking and hiding under the covers is entertaining."

I grin. "Well, I performed the pre-flight checks with my instructor. He climbed on board, and we lifted from the helipad and hovered behind the hangar. It was hot as hell, or maybe it was just nerves. Anyway, my flight suit was soaked in sweat. He had me fly a few laps around our planned touchdown point. Everything went perfect, and my nervousness went away. I think that was his plan."

"Makes sense."

"When we touched down, I felt calm and had everything under control. He asked me if I was ready to fly by myself. I remember my cheeks hurting from my grin. I was still scared but as ready as I would ever be. My confidence had returned, not that there wasn't a little fear. It felt like standing on a ledge. You don't want to take that leap, but you know it's the only way you'll ever fly."

"I love how you describe it."

"It was one of those life moments. I'll never forget it. My

instructor exited the helicopter, and as soon as he was a safe distance away, I lifted back on the lever that controls altitude. He told me to adjust for the difference in load. Without him in the seat beside me, the helicopter behaved differently, and I had to compensate for the difference in weight distribution. It rose faster than I anticipated and I nearly shit my pants."

Aiden huffs a laugh. "I doubt that."

"It was close, but actually, everything went smoothly after that. I hovered back and forth, all by myself, no instructor telling me what to do. It was hot as shit, and the one thing I remember was the death grip I had on the stick. Sweat beaded my brow and rolled down my face, but I didn't free up a hand to wipe it off. The sweat stung as it hit my eyes, and I couldn't see for a bit. All in all, I was so focused on what I was doing that I didn't have time to realize how amazing the whole thing was. I do remember one moment when I glanced over to the empty co-pilot seat and realized I was by myself. It's difficult to describe, but a mixture of pride and an intense thrill spread throughout my body. I may have said *Woohoo!* but don't you ever tell anyone that either."

"Surely, people in the tower heard. I'm sure you got ribbed for that."

"I would have if I'd remembered to activate the radio. It wasn't a perfect flight, but I did it. I was the first in my class to solo and finished first in my class."

There is something oddly soothing about sharing such a personal memory. It makes Aiden feel less of a stranger. Add to that, the very domestic task of doing laundry with him, and it feels normal.

Everything about Aiden feels … right. I don't know how to describe it other than to say it feels like he's always been in my life.

"Well," Aiden says, "you're pretty amazing in my book. Thanks for sharing that with me."

"I never really thought of it that way." I admit. "I guess I've done some pretty cool things."

"Is that something you always wanted to do? Not many women become pilots, let alone battle-tested combat pilots."

"As a little girl, I always wanted to fly helicopters. And I was a medevac pilot, not a combat pilot. There's a distinction."

"Is there?"

"Yeah, I didn't get to shoot at anything."

"Did you ever get shot at?"

Flashes of gunfire burst from a rocky scree. Two men stand up from behind a large boulder with an RPG. A smoke trail heads toward my position …

I'm not ready to answer that question.

"Well, I think it's amazing. There aren't many little girls that want to grow up to be helicopter pilots."

"I suppose not. What about your daughter? What does she want to do?"

"Callie wants to grow up and be a princess."

"I never wanted to be a princess. I always wanted to be the knight heading out to slay dragons."

He laughs. "I can see that. You're a badass."

"Well, I'm not sure about that."

He leans in close, crossing his arms in an obvious tactic to keep from reaching for me and pulling me close. I feel the need to be held by him. It's an undeniable force that tugs at me. Resisting is difficult.

"Trust me, Ariel, you're a fucking badass." His eyes spark with admiration, and I straighten my posture, loving his praise. He doesn't seem to be the kind of man to hand it out easily.

"Growing up, I never quite fit in. I wouldn't say I was a badass, more of an awkward kid."

"I bet you were a tomboy."

I laugh. "Definitely a tomboy; too rough and tumble for the girls, and too girly for the boys. It made for some pretty lonely summers."

"That's incredibly sad. A girl like you should have had plenty of friends."

"Well, I had friends, just not a lot of them. I'm not a real social person. All that time alone allowed me to read everything I could get my hands on about flying. When I was old enough, my dad let me take lessons in gliders. Once I mastered those, I knew I wanted to fly. As a teenager, I worked my ass off to pay for ground school.

While all my friends were getting their driver's license, I was getting my pilot certification."

"Impressive. You had spunk."

"Weird is what it was. I think it made me even more unapproachable. By then, all the girls had boyfriends except me. I think the boys found me intimidating, but I loved flying too much to stop. My dad was a wonderful man and supported my dreams. His only rule was that I had to earn the money to pay for it."

Aiden's warm eyes touch my heart. He's really invested in what I have to say. When was the last time I could say that about anyone? All the other men I've dated tend to ignore what I do for work. It always makes me feel like I shouldn't be proud of my accomplishments. It isn't that way with Aiden. He wants to know everything.

"Ouch. I can't imagine that was cheap." His eyes widen. "I have no idea what something like that costs, but I imagine quite a bit."

"Well, technically, he matched me dollar for dollar. He said if I stuck with it and showed him my grit—"

"Your grit?"

I smile. "Yeah, my dad was always saying shit like that. Anyway, I only had to earn half of what I needed. He was a really great man."

"I'm sorry," Aiden says. "I just realized …"

"It's okay. My dad lived a full life. He was just taken from me too soon."

"May I ask what happened?"

A private individual, I'm not the kind of person to share the intimate details of my life. With Aiden, the words flow. I tell him more in fifteen minutes than I've shared with my team, and I've been flying with Andrew and Larry for five years. Not that there's much to discuss during the course of our day, but we do have some downtime to chat.

Come to think of it, I know all about Andrew's wife, their three boys, the pug they got the kids for Christmas last year, and all the antics that brought. The same can be said for Larry's divorce several years ago and the string of women he dated after the dust settled.

He has plans to propose to his latest love, Cheryl, in a couple of months and is working out the details to make an epic proposal. It's crazy how much I know about them, but how little I share about my life.

Not that there's much to talk about. When not at work, I spend time kayaking in the calm waters of the Gulf, reading any number of different books, and donating my time teaching kids about flying. My life is full but lonely.

Aiden moves close and brushes a strand of hair off my cheek. "You don't have to talk about it if you don't want to. I didn't mean to pry. I'm just insanely interested in everything about you."

After changing, I let my hair hang loose about my shoulders. While flying, I tuck everything up into a tight bun, but in my off-time, I prefer to let it hang loose.

He runs his fingers through the long lengths, letting the curls wind around his fingers, while I shiver. The urge to lean against him and snuggle against his broad chest is overwhelming.

I glance toward the open door, and Aiden releases my hair.

"Sorry, it's hard keeping my hands to myself, but we should be safe. No one should be wandering around." He gives a deep sigh. "How about we check on Julian's progress? I'm sure everyone wants an update, and Duncan should be done with chow in a bit."

I glance at the time on the machine. We have nearly an hour before we need to switch things over.

"Yeah, that sounds like a plan."

Talk about my father and his death fades. I'm not ready to revisit those painful memories but appreciate the tenderness Aiden showed when asking.

We stop by the sickbay to check in on the others. Randall, Andrew, and Larry pulled stools around a gurney and are playing a game of cards. Aiden once again holds the door open for me, letting me go first. Rough and rugged, a gentleman hides inside of him. It makes him all the more attractive.

"What's the game?" I look at the pot, or what makes up the pot, and grin.

Andrew loves poker, but his wife doesn't believe in gambling.

They substituted coin and cash for odd objects scrounged from the stores of sickbay. Alcohol pads, Band-Aids, and 2x2 cotton bandages form a pile in the middle of the gurney. From the look of things, Andrew is losing his shirt.

"Seven-card stud," Larry says. "You want in?" He turns to Randall and gives a warning. "She may not look like it, but Ariel is a shark when it comes to cards. I think she cheats, although I've never caught her yet."

"Larry!" I laugh and shake my head. "Maybe I'm just lucky."

"Lucky my ass." Larry scoots to the side and pulls a nearby stool beside him. "You gonna join us?" He gestures to a box beside him filled with pretend cash. "The bank is open for business."

"Maybe later," I say.

Aiden stands beside me, not saying a word, although I catch the way his brows nearly climb up his forehead.

I turn to him. "You don't make it far in the Army without learning how to play. It passes the time in between getting shot at." By the way his eyes widen, I snap my mouth shut. I haven't shared the day my helicopter was shot down.

"Seriously, I don't know why that surprises me," he says, "but I'd love to play a little poker with you later."

I'm one hundred percent certain he doesn't mean playing with the guys, and it won't be with Band-Aids. My stomach does a little flip, thinking about a game of strip poker.

"Ariel and I are heading back to the bridge," Aiden says. "Any of you want to join us? I expect we'll be losing communications sooner rather than later. Anyone you need to call, this is the time."

Andrew pushes back from the makeshift card table and stretches. "I'd like to call home, make sure everyone is tucked in tight."

"We'll stay here," Larry says. "I already spoke to Cheryl, and someone's gotta hold down the fort." He gestures to the two injured crewmen who seem to be resting comfortably.

In the hall, I ask about the injured men. "How are they?"

"Jeffery will do fine. He's going to be in a bit of pain," Andrew says.

"You were worried about internal injuries. Are you still concerned?"

"I'll keep monitoring, of course, but I think he's out of the woods."

"What about Caleb?" Aiden's strong voice demands an update.

"We got him to wake and he seemed oriented. Answered basic questions, but there's no way to tell. My gut says it's nothing more than a bad concussion."

"But ..." Aiden peers over Andrew's shoulder at the still form of his crewman.

"If there's a head bleed, things can change."

"But it's been hours since the accident." Aiden twists his lips. "Shouldn't we know?"

"It can take days, to be honest. We'll do our best, but it's really out of our hands."

Andrew is an amazing flight nurse, but there are limits to what he can do. Aiden pushing him isn't helping.

"Hey," I say, interjecting into the conversation. "We've got a lot on our plates. How about we focus on what we can control?"

We walk to the command center, and I head straight for the weather station. Aiden takes Andrew to the communications center and shows him how to place a call. A glance at my phone reveals no service, but that's to be expected. There aren't cell towers out in the Gulf.

The radar doesn't look good. I pull up reports from NOAA, the national agency responsible for tracking severe weather, and take in a deep breath. Julian picked up speed along with power as it comes at the Alabama and Georgia coastlines.

"How's it look?" Aiden's warm breath flutters over my neck, bringing chills racing down my spine.

He places his hand on the small of my back as he leans over to stare at the display.

"Hitting us dead on. I've been in lots of hurricanes, but this will be the first time I've been in the eye of one."

"You and me both. Maybe we can pop out of hiding for a moment and soak it in."

"You want to go outside?" Night fell hours ago. There's little to see outside except for the driving rain. A few of the lights still shine down on the rig, and I cock my head. "Should those be turned off?" I point outside.

"Yeah, no reason to waste electricity with the rig evacuated. When we left, I would've shut everything down, but it doesn't make sense to have a blackout with the storm coming. Basic generators are still online."

"Oh. There's so much about oil rigs I don't understand."

"Well, we have time to give you a full tour of the crew facilities."

"There can't be much more than sleeping quarters and ..." My cheeks flush thinking about all the empty beds.

Aiden chuckles. "There are one or two things we can check out. I think boredom will be the biggest enemy."

Behind us, Andrew speaks to his wife and then to his sons. He makes sure everything is ready for the storm and that his wife has a list of who to call if they run into problems.

"Everything okay?" I ask when Andrew ends the call.

"Yeah, they were going to ride out the storm, but I convinced her to pack everyone up and head inland. Atlanta isn't that far. She's not happy about driving at night, but I think it's best. The outer rain bands haven't hit yet. I think she'll be safe."

"Good, I'm sure she'll feel better staying with family."

Andrew laughs. "No kidding. Nana is thrilled to have her grandbabies visit. She's not as happy about the dog but understands." He glances outside. "Looks like Julian is here."

"Not quite," Aiden says. "That's only a taste of things to come."

"Well, shit." Andrew pulls at his face and glances out the windows. "I think I prefer a room without a view." He glances at me, then shifts his gaze back to Aiden. "I'll catch you two later."

Without another word, Andrew leaves with a grin on his face. He shuts the door on the way out, sealing me in with Aiden.

Chapter Ten

Aiden

As Andrew leaves, I grasp Ariel's hand and pull her close. As expected, she places her palm against my chest, pushing me away.

"Aiden …" Her voice trembles, and uncertainty simmers in her eyes.

"I want you to listen for a second." I look into her eyes, take note of the trembling of her chin, and hate the way she shifts her gaze away from me.

Andrew is a perceptive man, and from the way he spoke to his wife, it's clear he understands love. If he has a problem with what's happening between me and Ariel, he wouldn't have left me alone with her. Andrew not only excused himself, but he closed the door behind him.

"I think we need to go back." Ariel shifts toward the door.

"Not until I have my say." I sense her panic and want to ease her fears.

"Look …" She's desperate to get away.

If I don't do something now, I'm going to lose her. No way in hell is that happening.

"You're going to listen, and that's not a request unless you're dying to go over my knee?" I arch a brow, testing those waters.

She doesn't pull back, but neither does she show the eagerness I hoped. That's okay; we'll have plenty of time to explore mutual fantasies later.

She gives a huff and stops pushing. "Okay, what do you want to say?" Her feistiness returns.

"This is how it goes." I suck in a deep breath. "If those guys are going to draw and quarter you for what's happening between us ..." I gesture between us, "then they need to do the same to me. I won't let them hang you for exploring what can't be stopped. There's nothing wrong with us getting together. What we've done, and what we'll do, we do together. If they have a problem with that, they can take it up with me."

"It's just ..." She pauses and hangs her head, dejected and defeated, but then her gaze pops to mine. "You don't get how hard it is to build up a reputation or how easy it is to lose it. If they see me sleeping around with someone I just met ..."

"Well, we haven't done that."

"But we will."

I love hearing those words on her lips. Tugging her close, I wrap my arms around her waist.

"Yes, luv, we will, but there's no reason to rush."

"But when we do, they're going to think—"

"Frankly, it's none of their business, and from what you've told me about yourself, you're not the kind of woman who sleeps around. Andrew is perceptive. He already suspects something is happening between us. So, why hide it? Why sneak around behind their backs when we're doing nothing wrong? I'm not ashamed of it. You shouldn't be either."

"Then why does it feel wrong?" Her eyes shimmer with an upwelling of tears. Not tears of sadness, but rather her frustration.

"That's a good question, but has nothing to do with us."

She chews her lower lip. "I guess maybe you're right."

"No maybe about it. You know I'm right. But why do you feel that way?"

"I guess it's a habit. I'm always fighting against stereotypes. If one of my classmates did well, it was because he was a natural, or earned it, or had worked really hard for it. If I did well, there were always whispers that I slept with the instructor or the instructor was sweet on me. I was never rewarded for being a natural, or earning it, or working hard. I think it affects things like this."

"And what is this, Ariel? What do you think this is?"

Her answer interests me because I have no idea what's happening. How did I fall this far, this fast, for a woman I don't know?

Some people believe in love at first sight. I'm not one of them, but I'm pretty sure we've stumbled into something amazing.

"What do you want me to say?"

"I want the truth because I won't have anything but truth between us. There's no reason to move forward if we're not honest with each other. I'll start if it helps."

She gives a nod. "It might."

"Okay, I'm a widower who lost his wife. I'm raising a daughter without her mother, and that leaves no time to date. My wife wanted nothing more than for me to fall in love again, but I didn't. I couldn't. I wasn't interested, and even if I was, I didn't have the time. Not that I was a saint, but the women I found never spent more than a night with me. It never felt right. I haven't done much of anything other than take care of my daughter. She's my everything. For the longest time, I thought that was enough. Then I saw you. I can't stop thinking about you, and not just about sex. I see a future I never thought possible. I don't understand what's happening, but I know I don't want it to end."

"That's incredibly sweet." The flush returns to her cheeks, and she can barely look at me.

I love the vulnerability that hints at.

"It may be, and there are a few things you should take away from that." I bend down and force her to look into my eyes. It's important to gauge whether she understands. "First off, I loved my wife, and I will always love the memories I have of her, but I'm not in love with her anymore. It hurts to say that, but I think she understood long before I ever did. Which brings me to the second part. I don't sleep around. This thing between us, it can't be a fling. I'm not in this for a one-and-done kind of thing, and I have a daughter to think about. If that scares you, this is the time to bail."

Her eyes widen and her lickable lips part on an exhale. I want to sweep down and kiss those lips, but I'm not done.

"Chemistry is a rare and beautiful thing. I don't understand it, except that from the moment I saw you, I felt a connection. No, not a connection. I'm fucking hungry for you, ravenous to claim every bit of you."

I move closer and look deep into her eyes. Her breathing is softer and the worried expression on her face melts into a sublime smile. The tension she carries in her neck and shoulders eases as my words seem to sink in. There's something about the way she looks at me that I've never seen in another woman and know I'll never see again. It's as if at that moment our souls connect and form a bridge.

"I don't know what to say." She tilts her face to stare at me. Her gaze darts between my eyes as if she seeks the truth of my words in their depths. I hope she finds what she needs.

"Don't say anything because I'm not done."

"Aiden …"

"Mmm, I love my name on your lips."

I bend down and barely brush her lips with mine. It's agony to pull back, but I do. If I don't, there will be no stopping what comes next. I grip her hands and run my thumb over the back of her hand, caressing her skin.

"In you," I begin, "I see a chance for a kind of love I never thought could exist. A connection strong enough to span space and time. And I see a love full of passion, explosive and unstoppable, the kind other people envy. It's not something I want to hide by sneaking around. It's the kind of thing I want to shout from the rooftops. And if they don't like it, if they judge you for exploring this with me, then they'll answer to me. It takes incredible courage to face your fears. I'll be beside you, defending you, every step of the way, but I have to tell you that I don't think you need that. Andrew knows, or suspects, and he left with a grin, not a frown. Do you think it's possible your friends might want something like this for you?"

"Wow." She shakes her head slowly back and forth. "I thought you were this rough and dirty oil rig guy, but you're a romantic."

I laugh. "Don't be fooled. I'm a filthy, dirty, kinky fucker in bed."

"I'm starting to realize that."

"Does that scare you?"

"I don't think I can be scared of anything with you."

"Music to my ears." I pull her close and allow my emotions to guide me. This isn't lust, although there's plenty of that. It's something I've missed in my life. "I need to feel your hands on me."

I place her palms flat against my chest, then let go, wondering if she will take the lead or pull away.

"Since we're sharing truths," she begins, "let me share mine."

"Okay." The heat of her palms sears my chest. I want to feel her soft skin against mine but will wait. Once she takes that final step, I'll take back control. Until then, she needs to come to me.

"I don't date."

"I find that surprising." I really do. This woman is a knockout, a rare natural beauty.

"Introvert, remember?"

She cracks a grin, and my heart swells at the rawness of her emotion. I get the feeling there are very few people she allows herself to be vulnerable with. To be included in that small number gives me hope.

I crack a smile. "You can be my introvert."

"Anyway, in my experience, when men find out what I do for a living, what I used to do, they run away. I seem to be intimidating to men, although I don't understand why. I'm not exactly ... aggressive when it comes to stuff like this."

"I kind of figured, and for the record, I'm perfectly cool with that. I have enough aggression for us both."

Her eyes crinkle. It's easy to joke with her, and I can do it while setting the tone for the kind of relationship I enjoy. In testing the waters, I'm beginning to realize how very well matched we can be.

"It's like with the boys and girls growing up. I don't keep female friends for long. They don't understand me. The men I work with are difficult. If I get too chummy, it gets awkward. Either they think I'm coming on to them, or they come on to me. After that, it's really uncomfortable. So, I tend to shy away from work relationships. Andrew and Larry are coworkers, and while I know a lot about their lives, they know very little about mine. It's like that with all the guys, and in my field, I'm usually the only woman. The few times I have been interested in a guy, once he figured out what I did, it became a competition. And not to blow my own horn, but it's kind of tough to measure up to a war decorated helicopter pilot."

"You're a war hero?" I love these tiny gems she brings up in casual conversation. Clearly, she thinks very little about her accomplishments. Her humility makes her even sexier, in my opinion.

She blushes. "Not sure about the hero part. I just did what had to be done. And technically, I was shot down, so ... not sure that's something to brag about."

"You got a medal for getting shot down?"

"Oh, no." She waves her hand. "I took a bullet for one of my crew."

She rushes on, not sharing, but it's a story I'll get out of her one day. My woman is not only hot, but fucking amazing, and a hero. Mary is going to love Ariel, and Ariel will be a great role model for my daughter.

I place my thumb under her chin and force her to face me. "For the record, you rock, but it doesn't intimidate me. As for who is and isn't in charge, I'm more the lead than follow kind of guy, and I'm very comfortable in that role, especially when it comes to sex."

The flush of her cheeks deepens two shades of red. She lowers her gaze, fluttering her lashes. It's easily the sexiest thing I've seen in years.

"I have no problems with a kickass woman by my side. The rest of the world can fuck themselves with whatever they want to think about that. You're mine and that means mine to take care of however I see fit."

And that's when I realize there will be a future between us because I can't envision a day without her in my life.

"You certainly know how to make a girl swoon."

"I also know how to make you scream."

"Hmm," she licks her lips.

We're going to kiss again, and hopefully do a whole lot more. Hot and swollen, my cock takes notice and strains against my zipper.

"Do you still think we need to head back?" I ask. "Because my quarters are just down the hall."

Chapter Eleven

Ariel

I CAN BARELY BREATHE AND DON'T KNOW WHETHER TO RUN TOWARD what Aiden offers or away. Either way, there will be regrets. I listen to every word he says, but I'm not sure if I believe any of it. He can simply be really good at getting women to jump into bed with him, and I'm the next fool to fall for it. Then again, everything he says could be the truth.

His words seem sincere, and the way he speaks about his late wife is touching. He makes no apologies for loving her, and he doesn't hide that he has a daughter. Most women find that a turnoff, but he put it out there first and foremost, giving me the chance to make a choice as to whether to proceed or not. I respect that.

In him, I see a chance for the kind of love that only exists in dreams and fairy tales.

Is it possible I can have a happily ever after?

Maybe he can be the knight who rides by my side as we slay dragons together? I like the idea of that.

Insecurity plagues me, and I hate the weakness that implies. A lifetime of self-doubt and never quite measuring up leaves me terrified of being used. I also have a wretched track record with men. My heart says to go for it. My gut tells me to run.

He turns that serious look of his on me. Warm, sizzling eyes bore into me as he waits for me to make a choice. If I go to his room, sex will follow. It's an eventuality I crave with the fiercest hunger, but I also have much to lose.

He doesn't seem fazed by the risks to my reputation, although he makes no bones about standing by my side. He will protect me; of that, I have no doubt.

Obliterating the space between us, he places his hands on my bare arms and runs them along my skin, raising goosebumps and lighting my nerves on fire. The electricity of his touch jumpstarts my heart, and I imagine what his lips will feel like if his hands feel this good.

He folds me into his arms, wrapping his bulk around me as he smooths my hair. It's a tender embrace, full of passion but more comforting than anything I've ever felt.

In his arms, I feel safe, as if the weight of the world settles on his shoulders rather than mine. How long have I been the only one I can count on? There's no one in my life with whom to share my burdens, and it would be nice not to have to walk alone.

His touch seems to bring me back to life and revive what I lost. Hell, I didn't even realize I lost anything. But there are pieces inside of me that are shattered. Aiden gives me hope and a promise to help me put everything back together again. I can lean on him and know he's strong enough to bear my burdens.

His words are precious gifts, and his laughter the remedy I need to ease my fears. He's a stranger who is quickly becoming more … not a lover, but one on the cusp of becoming just that.

I lean my head against his chest and breathe in his musky scent. He smells of strength and purpose.

With slow and deliberate exploration, I run my hands up his arms. Sculpted muscles pass beneath my fingers as I trace the hard ridges of tendons held taut with strength. In his arms, I feel safe; if that's the right word for the sensations rushing through my body.

Pressed up against every inch of him, my body awakens, becoming more alive than I've felt in a very long time.

What will it be like to have something like this in my life? To be safe within a man's arms, protected, and not always left to fend for myself? I want this, and maybe those desires have me rushing too fast. The feeling can't be stopped.

No matter what my rational mind says, this feels right. I want to be wrapped in his arms forever, with every chance the universe is kind enough to grant. But I'm not ready to take that final step.

"I think we need to change out the laundry." I expect him to argue and try to persuade me to head to his room, but he huffs a soft laugh instead.

"We can do that."

I peek up at him, happy to see a smile on his face instead of a frown, but still feel the need to apologize. "Sorry, I'm just not ready."

He lifts me against his chest and kisses the crown of my head. "Never apologize for needing to take a step back."

"You don't mind? You're not upset?"

He shakes his head. "Luv, we've got all the time in the world." He releases me and opens the door. "Let's take care of the laundry, see what Duncan has whipped up, and check on the others. We've got another couple of hours before Julian really gets kicking."

I glance out the window, mesmerized by the fury outside. "It's incredible, isn't it? I almost wish it was daylight so I could see the storm better." I reach over the counter to place my palm against the glass. Deep vibrations shake beneath my palm as the wind whips and lashes at the thick glass. "It's a little more frightening in the dark."

"I'm sure we'll have plenty of time to watch the storm."

His eyes are not on the window behind me but rather roving over my body. The desire brimming in his eyes and vibrating in the space between them isn't something he chooses to hide, but neither does he force the inevitability of our connection.

I appreciate that.

Asking to take a breather from the overwhelming heat between us isn't easy and could be met with any number of responses. Like everything else, he surprises me with a gentleness I don't expect. Aiden is genuine, a gentleman and a rogue; he embodies both sides of the perfect coin.

We return to the laundry, and he helps me switch the clothes from washer to dryer. He gives me a wink as he pulls my black bra and silk panties from the washer.

"I'm not sure what's sexier ..." He makes a point of holding up my black panties.

"I'm almost afraid to ask." Normally, a strange man holding my undergarments would make me squirm, but with Aiden, I don't feel weird about it.

"Well, the mystery of what you wear under your flight suit is no longer a secret. I have to say I had a few inappropriate fantasies about that when you first hopped out of your helicopter."

"I guess men really do think about sex all the time."

"Constantly," he says with a chuckle. "Nonstop, actually. Do you know what I'm thinking about now?"

"I'm pretty sure it has nothing to do with the laundry." I grab for my panties, but he yanks them out of my reach.

His deep laugh rumbles through the room, bringing a smile to my face and warming my heart. He is an easy man to be around because he holds very little back. A genuine individual, he carries a smile on his face most of the time.

"Well, once the laundry is finished, I can give you back your clothes." I hold out my hand for my panties.

"No," he says, shaking his head, "that's just it."

"What?"

"The answer to what's sexier."

"My clothes." I flex my fingers, demanding he hand over my panties.

He gives me a look, one that says he'll do so only when, and if, he decides. "The fact I know you're not wearing anything beneath my clothes is a fucking turn-on."

I gesture at the baggy clothing. "Your shirt hangs down to my knees, and I had to roll up the waistband of your sweatpants and tie it into a knot to keep them from slipping off my hips. I'm pretty sure there's nothing sexy about what I'm wearing."

"Ah, see, that is where you're entirely wrong."

"You don't say." The infectiousness of his grin makes me smile with him.

"I know it for a fact, and I'm a bit jealous."

"Of what?"

"The fact that my clothes get to touch things I haven't had a chance to touch yet. It's driving me crazy."

"I think you'll live." We banter easily. I've never felt this comfortable around a man before.

Every time he looks at me, he steals every bit of my breath, taking it into himself, where he holds it close like a precious gift. It's the same way when he kisses me, and I want more of that now, despising my decision to slow things down. The entire world seems to stop and hover on what he will do or say next.

"Oh, I'll suffer through, but I'm not sure life is worth living if I can't touch you."

Even his gentle teasing soothes me like he eases the tension wound up inside of me and unties all the knots that bind me inside my head. He promises freedom I've never known.

"Aiden …"

Is this what falling in love is like? Can it happen this quickly?

I can count on my fingers the number of hours—hours!—I've known him, and yet he's already forged a path into my heart and made a home for himself.

He makes a show of handing over my panties, letting his fingers caress my hand as he does.

If this is love, it's a story I never want to end. This is that connection others share, a bond I've only ever observed from the outside looking in. I long for it, and now that it might be within my grasp, I'm terrified of losing it.

"Don't worry, I'll suffer in silence, but now you'll know what I'm thinking every time I look at you." His wink is a force of devastation.

"I don't think I can forget." I toss the rest of the clothes into the dryer. "How about we find the others?"

"Hun, they're not lost. We know exactly where they are."

"Ha, ha, you know what I mean."

"Yes, luv, I know exactly what you mean. Come. I say chow, and then it's time for a tour of the place. Don't want you wandering about and tripping over something dangerous."

"Is there anything really dangerous in the crew area?"

"Actually, no, but I'm sure you'll want to do more than sit in the sickbay. We have a gym and several lounge areas, the chow hall, of course."

"It must be a strange life, living out here." There's nothing comfortable, or homey, about the crew quarters. It feels barren. I don't like it.

"It's only two weeks at a time. The other two weeks are suburbia normal, full of driving my daughter to school, soccer, tumbling, dance, and all the fun stuff."

"Who takes care of her when you're here?"

"Her grandmother."

"Ah, that's wonderful that your mom helps you out."

"Not my mother."

"Oh."

There's more than a daughter in his life. The ghost of his dead wife lingers in her mother raising her granddaughter. My brows pinch together, worried how that might change things.

He grins, one of those infectious looks which takes the sudden pit of worry and banishes it to the dark depths.

"I think you'll like Mary. She's dying to meet you."

"Me?"

"Yeah, you."

"How would she know about me?"

"I called to check in on them. Mary is highly intuitive."

"Um…"

He centers the weight of his mesmerizing gaze on me and shatters my defenses. "I know what you're thinking, and you need to stop it. Mary is a saint, and she probably already has our wedding planned."

"It's a little weird talking about your …"

"You mean my dead wife's mother planning her son-in-law's wedding?"

"Well, yeah …"

He makes a dramatic sigh. "Whew! I thought you were worried about the marriage part."

Before I can react, he has my hand in his and leads me through the hall.

Chapter Twelve

Aiden

I DECIDE DUNCAN OUTDID HIMSELF WITH DINNER. I EXPECT something mediocre, barely palatable. Instead, the man creates a five-star, mouth-watering feast.

Duncan whipped up an amazing treat of shrimp alfredo, Caesar salad, baked potatoes, breadsticks, and even cheesecake for dessert. It isn't a fancy meal, but far more satisfying than I anticipated.

Andrew and Ariel sit with us, silently clearing their plates. The food is so good, no one is talking.

"I think you're in the wrong job," I say to my friend. "We need to change your position to galley cook."

Duncan snorts. "Like hell. There's no way I'm cooking for a hundred needy mouths. No one is ever satisfied, and everyone wants it done their way. I don't take requests either. You eat what I make, and that's that."

"Well, I'm stuffed." Ariel clears her plate and takes it to the sink in the galley to wash. "I agree with Aiden, that was easily the best meal I've had in ages. You may have missed your calling as a chef. It's a shame the Gulf has stolen you away."

"Chef's don't make half what I make out here, and who says I'm not a culinary wonder during my time on shore?"

"Are you?" I say with a playful wink.

"No," he says, "maybe I just like the view?"

"Is that why you're here?"

"It's a nice view."

I laugh. We truly have one of the best views on the planet, but I know it's the money that brings Duncan back year after year.

There aren't many jobs where you can make good money working two out of every four weeks. Granted, those two weeks are back-breaking work, but it makes the time off worth it.

"True," I grab my plate and clear Duncan's. "You sit. He who cooks does not clean."

"Well, ain't you being a sweetheart and all," Duncan says. "Looks like someone has you on your good behavior."

I give Duncan the eye and a sharp shake of my head to silence him. Duncan rolls his eyes. He doesn't miss a thing.

"You seriously don't want to go there," I say in a whisper. "Not unless what you're going to say is thank you for helping out with the dishes."

Ariel's flight nurse gives a snort. "Well, I don't work for you, so you can't tell me to shut up." Andrew waves his fork toward Ariel. "It's clear as day what's happening between you two."

"Lower your voice, asshole." I glance at Ariel, not sure if she hears, hoping the sound of running water drowns out Andrew's words. Leaning close, I place the dishes back down on the table. "Look, I don't want us to have a problem, but you keep your nose out of it and your opinions to yourself. She doesn't need any shit from you."

"Ain't no problem." Andrew doesn't flinch and leans in, closing the gap. This isn't a man who backs down from a challenge. He does lower his voice, however. "I'm putting my nose in it if only to tell you this."

"And what would that be?"

"If you fuck with her, if this is just a game to you, know that I will find you and fuck you up."

"Protective much?" I lean back, impressed, but I'm not intimidated by Andrew.

"What would you do if someone hurt her?" Andrew fires back.

"I'd rip his head off." There's no thought required to answer that question.

Andrew gives a curt nod. "Well, good that we understand each other then. Don't hurt her, and you and I will be fine."

Duncan gives a snort. "You don't need to worry about Aiden. He's one of the good guys. Your lady's in good hands."

"We'll see about that." Andrew slaps his plate on the stack of dishes and shoves them toward me. "Go help her with the dishes. Duncan and I will relieve Randall and Larry so they can eat."

"Should we bring Jeffery something?" Duncan asks. "Guy's got to be starving by now."

Andrew shakes his head. "I'm still not a hundred percent sure there's nothing going on in his gut. He can go without food a little bit longer."

Duncan pushes off from the table. "Looks like you've got a minute alone with her, boss. Don't fuck it up."

"She's not going to like that you're talking about her." I glance at Ariel's back as she reaches for a pot and sets it into a soapy sink. I'm not certain, but I think she's humming.

"Well, you'd have to be an idiot to miss it," Andrew says. "Tell her not to worry."

"Right." That's exactly what I won't do.

Ariel expressed concerns over what her crew thinks and how her reputation might suffer. I admit, although ruefully, that not taking her to my quarters was the better idea. Not that sitting next to her during that dinner and not touching her wasn't hell, but maybe now I don't have to worry about it.

I grab the stack of dishes and join her while Duncan and Andrew leave. At least everyone is keeping to the buddy rules, even if they did switch things up. Placing the dishes down on the dirty side of the sink, I rub Ariel's shoulders.

"You want the good news or the bad?" I ask.

She glances at me. "I always like taking the bad news first, but if you're going to tell me they know about us, don't bother. None of you are good at whispering, or using your inside voices, especially when you're all growly, possessive, and protective."

"You heard?"

"How could I not?"

"It seemed like you didn't."

"What was I going to do, turn around and join in while the three of you compared dick sizes?"

"Dick sizes?" I love her filthy mind, so damn sexy.

"Yes. I swear I don't know how men get anything done when you're all standing around trying to figure out whose dick is bigger. Seems like a waste of time."

"That Andrew fellow is a good friend. Not sure I want to step wrong around him. And for the record, my dick is the biggest."

She laughs at that, a genuine, honest laugh. It's easily the most perfect thing I've ever heard. She recovers quickly, though.

"You'd regret it. He's ex-military, C-CATT for eight years and SOST-SOCCET after that."

"See cat and soft socks? What the fuck is that?" I dig deep into the muscles of her neck, loving the way my fingers bring soft moans to her lips.

"Critical Care Air Transport Team," she says with a grin, "and Special Ops Surgical Team, or SOST."

"You said soft socks." I dig into the tension girding her shoulders, and she moans softly. "I like making you moan."

"Then keep doing that. It feels amazing."

"So, soft socks?"

She giggles. "Please don't ever let Andrew hear you call it that. It's Special Ops Surgical Team, Special Ops Critical Care Evacuation Team: SOST-SOCCET."

"Yeah, you military love your abbreviations. So, he's ex-military too?"

"Most of us are."

"Well, that badass is protective of his teammate."

She spins around and places her soapy hands on my cheeks.

"Yeah, but don't let that scare you off. I'm looking forward to a whole-body rub now. Your fingers are magical."

"Now that is music to my ears." I lean in and brush my lips against hers. "So, you're okay with them knowing?"

She shrugs. "I'd rather not have my personal business on public display, but the cat's out of the bag, and I refuse to act like I'm ashamed. I'm okay with it."

"Wow, you really do have balls. After what you said earlier …"

She grips her tits and gives them a squeeze. "See these?"

"Hun, that's my entire universe right there."

"Well, you're right. I have balls. They're called tits and are easily bigger and badder than any man's balls. I'm a private person, and while I would prefer this thing between us remain private, that's no longer possible. The only thing to do now is to suck it up and own it. Unless Andrew has you running scared?"

I know one thing I want her to suck.

"I'm not scared of a guy with soft socks who sees cats." I reach out and snap my arm around her waist, pulling her in close to plant a kiss on her lips.

The door to the galley bangs open.

"Eww, get a room guys!" Larry makes a beeline for the food and plops down on a stool. He shovels food onto his plate and grabs a breadstick. "It's getting fierce out there." He pokes the end of the breadstick toward the windows and says nothing else about our kiss.

It's pitch-black outside, but the entire rig hums with the energy of the storm and the crashing of the waves against the support pylons. I feel the vibrations through my boots and despite the thick glass, the howling of wind can't be ignored.

Ariel pushes me away, a flush bright on her cheeks. She might have said she was okay with everyone knowing, but public displays of affection hit her triggers. I make a mental note to keep my hands to myself, at least in front of the others.

"How are Jeffery and Caleb doing?" I turn to Larry to ask about my injured crewmen.

"Jeffery is awake and in pain. Caleb is in and out but lucid when we wake him up. He hates it when I pinch his toes, but it could be worse."

"Thank you for taking care of them."

"Of course. Hate to have to do it for anyone, but it's the best job in the world."

Randall shoves open the door and takes a deep breath. "Smells damn good. Duncan did this?"

"Yes," I say with a smile. "He's been holding out on us."

Randall joins Larry at the table and loads his plate. I return to help Ariel with the dishes, grabbing a towel to begin drying.

I spend the next twenty minutes in bliss, standing beside her doing something as mundane as the dishes. It makes me ache for more moments like this with her in the days, weeks, and years to come.

How is it possible that after a few hours, I've fallen so far?

I don't understand it. Don't care to, really, but something magical is happening. And I don't care that I can't touch her the way I want. Standing beside her, I touch her in any number of different ways, brush the back of her hands, push back the hair from her face, and knead the knots in her shoulders.

All of it is nonsexual and yet the most sensual thing I've experienced in a very long time. Her warmth seeps into me, comforting me with the promise of more, and all without me saying a word or even touching me back. She belongs next to me, and I belong next to her.

Ariel finishes the last pan and stands there with soap covering her hands, tiny bubbles cling in small clumps over her delicate fingers. A serene expression covers her face as if she floats in a moment of serenity.

With a half-smile and eyes that promise an exciting future, she turns and takes the towel out of my hand. Slowly, she wipes at the soapy bubbles clinging to her hands, then folds the towel in half. With her gaze latched onto me, she rises on tiptoes to chastely kiss my lips.

It's the best gift I've ever received, her reaching out to me.

I wrap my arms around her slender waist and pull her close.

Behind me, Larry clears his throat, and Randall gives a snort. I don't kiss her the way my body demands, but I do kiss her with possession and promise.

"Come," I say, "let me take you on a tour of your home for the next couple of days."

As I lead her out of the room, Randall gives a low chuckle. "You two behave, ya hear?"

Chapter Thirteen

Ariel

I ENJOY THE TOUR AIDEN PROVIDES OF THE CREW QUARTERS. IT'S interesting to see what life is like on a rig, but what I really want to see are the working parts of an oil rig. Unfortunately, that isn't happening with Julian's arrival. We stand by a window looking out over the ocean.

Julian's violent fury rages outside, whipping up the sea, and making the rain fall sideways and gust upwards. The normally calm Gulf waters surge with waves cresting in the dark. I peer into the maelstrom, trying to make out details.

"It's impressive, isn't it?" Aiden tugs me close.

I lean against Aiden's firm chest and grip his wrist. He slings his arm over my shoulder and I snuggle into his embrace, feeling safe and secure. A deep breath brings his musky scent, filling my senses.

"I feel the waves hitting the supports. It's weird, like a low growl and incessant vibration. Is it always like that?"

"Not usually," he says. "The Gulf has some of the calmest waters on the planet. As Duncan said, the view is pretty awesome. We do get waves, but they're generally of pretty low intensity.

Sometimes, you can feel them as they sweep past the rig, but nothing like this."

"I love the ocean. It's calm and serene one moment and then violently powerful the next. It makes me feel insignificant."

He tightens his grip. "You're anything but insignificant."

"What happens during storms? Do you keep working through them, or pull everyone inside?"

"Guess it depends on the storm. Lightning is a concern, of course, and if it's bad enough to affect visibility, we stop operations, but you know how it is out here. Squalls kick up, blow through, and it's gorgeous afterward. I imagine it's much different for you in the air."

"It's beautiful," I say with a sigh. "From horizon to horizon, nothing but the ocean beneath my feet and blue sky overhead. I love chasing storms, or dodging them as it may be. Lightning is not my favorite though."

"You have no idea how kickass you are, do you?"

"It's a job. Much like any other, it has fun parts and boring parts. I'm sure it's not much different for you. I bet it can get pretty boring here."

"It's a little less boring with you in my arms." He nuzzles the side of my neck and makes my skin tingle with a fluttering of kisses which land with a nibble to my earlobe. "You're incredible."

"I don't know about incredible, but I love what I do."

"Do you ever miss the military?"

I breathe out a sigh. "I do. There's a camaraderie there that isn't quite the same in civilian life. Everyone fights the same mission. You're tight with those you work with, or should be."

"You weren't?"

"I was and wasn't. My crew respected me, and the soldiers were always polite and respectful."

"But?"

"I was female. I missed out on all the dick-measuring contests."

He laughs at that comment. "I bet you did."

"That's a difficult bridge to navigate. I was one of the guys, but most definitely not a guy. Does that make sense?"

"You're a hero. I bet that brought respect."

"It did, but I was still always left on the sidelines. Included because they had to, but only as an afterthought. It's hard to explain. It sounds like I'm complaining, which I'm not. I had a great time as a Warrant Officer, best job in the world."

Until I took a bullet, became a hero, and was medically discharged for my service and sacrifice. It was a difficult thank you to accept.

I firm my chin and remind myself that I have no regrets. My life is good, and I'm still flying. Not everyone can say the same. Reggie died in that crash, as did others.

I need to shift topics before a boatload of unhealthy emotions claw their way to the surface.

"Do you have any idea how high the waves can get?"

"Do you really want to know the answer to that?" The heat of Aiden's breath whispers against my neck.

"Why?" I spin around and thread my fingers in with his.

"Answer the question. Do you really want to know?"

From the look on his face, I pause to consider, but damn, I need to know now.

"Yes."

"Well, no one really used to know how big waves got inside hurricanes, all the sensors used to get ripped off their moorings, but the Naval Research Laboratory has these new wave/tide gauges which are submerged and anchored to the seafloor. It's a lot of science I don't understand, but they can measure wave heights now with surprising accuracy."

"And?"

"When Hurricane Ivan passed through, they measured waves nearly a hundred feet tall."

"You're fucking kidding me? That's like freak waves though. Not normal hurricane waves."

He snickers. "Good thing we don't have a swear jar here."

I punch him playfully. After eight years in the Army and three tours to the desert, I can hold my own with the worst offenders.

"How strong was Ivan?" I ask.

"Category 4 and waves of that height are more common than people originally thought. True, it's not normal, but they happen more than you want to know."

He's right about that, especially since we're sitting in the middle of the Gulf, hunkering down while Julian blows right over us.

"Wow," I say, "and to think that Julian is Ivan's bigger, badder cousin."

"Yup."

"And you're sure we're safe?"

"As safe as we can be." He spins me around and puts his hands on my hips. He dips down, bending his knees until he's eye level with me. "Look, these things are built to withstand the storm of the century."

"Thanks, that helps." I give a shaky nod. "Tell me about the rig. Help me keep my mind off things."

"How much do you want to know?"

"Everything." I lean against him. "Tell me everything."

With his arms wrapped around my waist, I listen as he talks about his job, the people who work for him, and how much he enjoys what he does. I asked him to tell me about the rig, but he does so much more. He shares pieces and parts of his life. Meanwhile, Julian roars.

I lean my head against his chest and a yawn slips out.

"Hey, you have to be exhausted," he says. "How about we head back, check in with the others, and grab some shut-eye?"

"What time is it?"

He glances at his watch. "2 a.m."

"Wow." I suppress another yawn. "I'd like to head back to the Control Room and see if we can radio back. If we haven't lost coms yet, we will soon."

He grips me tight before releasing me. "Your military is showing."

"Huh?"

"Coms," he says. "It's not a common word."

"I guess not."

"I never asked why you left. Did you just finish up your obligation?"

"Kind of. My commitment was up. I thought about re-upping, but after the crash …"

"Where you took a bullet for a patient—"

"Where I did what anyone would've done. Anyway, I was medically retired from the Army after the injury."

"Shit, you're something else, luv. I see how men can be intimidated around you."

"Are you?"

"I'm impressed, not intimidated. And like I said, in my relationships, I tend to be a bit traditional."

"Bossy, you mean," I tease.

"You don't seem to be running from it."

"I'm not, but I love what I do. I'm not going to give it up to be a domestic goddess."

He roars with laughter, then grips my waist and spins me back to him. "Is that what you think?"

"Well…"

"Hun, I'm raising a kickass daughter, who I hope will become whatever she wants in life. My mother-in-law is a phenomenal woman, as fierce and loving as they come. Strong women don't scare me, and I'd never diminish what you've done, or keep you from doing what you love."

"But, you said …"

"That I'm dominant in bed, but that doesn't mean I'm a domineering asshole. What kind of men have you been dating?"

I look at him, falling into the depths of his baby blues, and sigh. "Evidently the wrong kind."

"Well, time to fix that." He takes my hand in his. "Come, let's call base, check on the others, and get some shut-eye."

"Shut-eye?"

"Surprised?"

"Well, I just assumed …"

"I like the direction of your thoughts, and while I'd love to explore your body and learn all about your scars, I've had a long day. If the shit hits the fan with Julian, I'd rather face it with a couple of hours of sleep under my belt."

"You're nothing like I expected."

"How's that?"

"Most men wouldn't want to sleep. They'd be pushing for sex."

He takes both my hands in his again. "Never think for a minute I don't want that. I can't wait to sink into your wet heat or discover if your pussy tastes as good as I've been imagining all night. I fully intend to have you screaming my name."

"Wow!" His words make my heart pound. "That's more like what I expected."

"Well, we have plenty of time for all of that."

"Do we?"

"We have all the time in the world, luv. I have no intention of ever letting you go."

The profoundness of his words spins in my head. It's as if I've found a way home. My entire life I've had to stand up for myself, reaching for impossible goals, shattering them, and then looking left and right for someone to share them with.

In those moments, I always stood alone.

That's the way of the world for a woman who seeks the kind of dreams I chase. To think I found a man who's not only not intimidated by my career choice, but embraces it, is a dream.

Is it possible a woman like me can find my happily ever after? Can an ex-Army helicopter pilot also be the princess saved by her prince?

I've never been a romantic. Never played into those dreams. But Aiden makes me believe I can have everything.

And that scares me silly.

Chapter Fourteen

Aiden

NOT TAKING ARIEL TO BED IS THE HARDEST DECISION I'VE EVER made in my life. My entire body screams to slake my lust and satisfy my thirst for the pleasures she promises. Stunningly beautiful, courageous, and fierce, I've never met a woman who hits all my buttons.

Samantha was different. She was sweet and soft, yielding and resilient, the perfect complement to my take-charge attitude. Ariel is everything Samantha wasn't, and yet perfect in many of the same ways.

Making a promise to Samantha I never intended to keep was hard. It feels like breaking a vow. Lying to Samantha gutted me on the deepest level, but she saw something I couldn't see. Her love transcends her time on earth and gives me permission to let her go. That shows her grace and the depths of her love. Samantha always knew how to call my bluff and beat my bullshit.

She paved the path to my future happiness by making me promise something I couldn't stomach. Always wiser than I was, and forceful in her gentle nature, she gave me an impossible gift.

How many men would find love, not once but twice in their lifetime?

I thank her for that wisdom now.

Things with Ariel move with the same relentless determination as the storm raging its fury outside. We aren't in control of the events surrounding us, the passion brewing between us, or the eventuality of our fate. Our worlds collided with explosive force, and who knows what will become of us in the aftermath.

Irresistible, undeniably amazing, Ariel is something I never expected. That makes me cautious, even when my body tells me to charge ahead, claim what I want, and never let her go.

Moving too fast, however, could be the worst mistake of my life.

So, I hold back.

I do so because my eye is on the bigger prize. A quick fuck might feel good. It would definitely ease the heavy ache in my balls, but I risk losing something precious: a future with an amazing woman, not to mention fulfilling that damn promise I gave to my late wife.

I see it now.

Samantha's love remains and fills me with amazing memories, but she carved out a place for someone new. Her insight into a future she would never share with me leaves me speechless and profoundly at peace.

Every day since her passing, my soul ached. Some of that pain muted over the years, but only because life continued without her. Our daughter needed to be raised. Groceries didn't buy themselves, and little girls who wished to feel the undying love of both their parents sometimes needed more from the one they had left.

I fill both roles as best I can, making my daughter's life as full as possible, and with each day, a part of me dies inside.

Samantha knew this would be my future. As her death approached, she hoped for a life I couldn't imagine, and she did the one thing I never could. She gave me permission not only to live and find love again, but to do so without guilt.

I never fully understood the gift she gave in forcing me to honor her dying wish until now.

That knowledge rests in my arms. It's present in the tightness of Ariel's grip as I lead her to the Control Room. It echoes in my heart as she calls back to base, getting updates on the storm and reporting our status. It's in the warmth of her eyes as she looks at me when she thinks I'm not looking. It's in the softness of her body when it wraps around mine. And it's in the strength of her mind, her determination to face incredible odds and not only succeed but thrive.

The woman is fierce, independent, and incredibly resilient. Little did I know when I anchored her to me during our walk from the helideck, how prophetic that moment would become. In every way, she is the one I want, and I'm never letting her go.

She gives another yawn. "You know, I think it's time to catch some z's. If anything happens …"

"It won't." I pull her deep into my embrace. "Let me show you to your quarters."

She looks up at me and blinks with those forever-long lashes. "Actually, the idea of sleeping alone is a little spooky. Do you think I can crash with you?"

That will be the sweetest torture.

"Do you really expect me to keep my hands to myself?" There's no way to share a bed with her and not take her the way my body demands. It isn't just a bad idea; it's courting disaster.

"It's okay if you don't want to. I just don't want to sleep alone, but I have to say that I'm not ready for anything else. I've never had a one-night stand, and I would rather not start now."

Dear lord, is that what she thinks?

"There's no one night anything about this. I'd love to hold you in my arms, even if it kills me to do so."

Danger. Danger.

This is going to be a disaster. I should say no, but I can't make her sleep alone, not after she admits to being scared.

"Thanks, that means a lot to me."

"Come." I take her hand and lead her to my quarters.

With her shyly ducking her head, I pull back the covers of my bed. "It's a twin bunk, gonna be a tight fit."

Her eyes widen at that comment, and then she laughs. "Sorry, it's just when you said that ..."

"Oh, I know exactly how it sounded, but Scout's honor. I'll be a true gentleman."

"Since it's going to be a tight fit," a sly smile ghosts across her face, "maybe it's best if I take the edge. I'd hate for you to fall out."

I slap my thigh with that one. "Hun, there'll be no falling out. I can God-damn-guarantee-that. And I'm a gentleman. I'm totally pinning you to that wall."

She gives me a look. "Is that a promise?"

I can't wait to pin her to the wall, bend her over the desk, lay her out on the bed, send her to her knees, and do all manner of nasty things. I gulp with all those images racing in my head.

"Always," I say, "but beware of promises."

"How's that?"

"Because I tend to keep them." For the first time in years, I can finally say that and have it be true.

"I hope so. I have a feeling I'm in for an education."

"You have no idea." I give a light smack to her ass. "Now, climb in."

I wait for her to climb into bed before turning out the light. We go to bed fully clothed. Not a choice I relish, but it seems to make her feel more comfortable. There's a second, more important reason. In case of emergency, not that I expect anything to happen, if we have to get up in a hurry, it'll be one less thing to worry about.

There is a little rearranging before we find a position where we're both comfortable. I wrap my large frame around hers and drape an arm over her waist while she faces the wall. With my burdens lifted, my heart lighter, and my thoughts a frustrated mess, I finally drift off to sleep.

Chapter Fifteen

Ariel

MORNING FINDS ME BATHED IN A GRAY LIGHT PEEKING THROUGH THE window and Aiden's erection poking me in the back. I try to stretch until I remember we share a twin bed. Any movement will press against his very pressing need.

Was it wrong telling him I need to slow down? And really, how slow is it to sleep in a man's bed who I met the day before. Sure, there was no sex, but there's been so much more.

Things have been said. Scary things. Mentions of forever and love.

Love!

How can I love a man I've known for less than a day? And he said something similar to me.

We're lust drunk.

That must be the explanation. We should have sex, just to get it out of the way. Maybe then, some of the intensity between us will ease up a bit and I can find room to breathe.

Only, I don't want more space between us. In his arms, I feel secure, safe, sheltered, and at peace. I feel each of these individually and together. It's a wonderful, welcoming bliss.

"Hun, don't you dare move." His growly voice forces me to stillness.

"You awake?"

"Yes, and very hard."

I giggle. "Problem?"

My body is on high alert. Everything about Aiden affects me on a gut level. It's as if my senses are magnified in his presence. The aroma of his sexy musk percolates through the air and deepens my breaths. His electric touch lifts the fine hairs on my arms. His breath whispers in my ears, promising delicious things to come … if I allow it. And his husky voice destroys me in the most wonderful way imaginable.

And isn't that exactly what I want? Is there any question about whether I want to have sex with him?

Last night, I needed the serenity of being held in his arms, a pause from our sizzling chemistry. Today? I need something else entirely.

"It's only a problem if you intend on teasing me with that fine ass," he says with a rumble that vibrates through my chest.

"You want me to stop?" I arch my back and wiggle against his hard length. "You sure about that?"

He grips my hip and clenches the skin. "Don't start something you don't intend to finish, or I will put you over my knee and redden that pert ass of yours."

"Promises, promises," I tease.

But maybe it isn't the wisest thing to push Aiden. He might go through with his threats. I've never been spanked before. It seems incredibly deviant and insanely exciting.

I quiet down and don't move, even though my entire body thrums for more.

He presses his lips to the side of my neck. The gentle kiss takes away my words, silences my thoughts, and sets every sense on high alert. This is happening.

His hand glides down the curve of my hip and circles around to tickle the back of my knee. Ever so slowly, his fingers move along the inside of my leg and toward the juncture of my thighs, where a needy throb takes root.

Holding back the low moan escaping from my throat is an impossibility, so I don't even try. I'm both thankful, and annoyed, we're both fully clothed.

"I take it that's a yes? Or, do you want me to stop?"

"Yes." My hips rock with need.

"Yes, you want me to stop?"

I shake my head. "No."

"Then yes to what, luv? What is it you want?"

He's going to make me say it. I flip around and stare into his amazing eyes, satisfied to find my hunger mirrored in his lustful gaze.

"You know what I want," I say.

"Do I?" He arches a brow. "I wouldn't want to assume. Maybe you want me to braid your hair. For the record, I'm proficient in all manner of French braiding. I have my certificate from Callie hanging on my wall."

"I bet you do." I giggle.

"But that's not what you want, is it?"

"No."

He stares at me and arches a brow.

"Are you really going to make me say it?"

His eyes pinch with mirth. "Oh, you damn well bet I am. If only to see you squirm."

I'm already squirming. The ache between my legs needs attention.

"I want you." I trace the line of his jaw and run my finger over the fullness of his lips. His smile eliminates whatever resistance I have left. Although, to be honest, I've already made my decision. I want him deep inside of me.

"Now that is music to my ears." He flicks back the covers, and I gasp with surprise. "You're wearing entirely too much clothing."

We went to bed fully dressed, a concession he made when my uncertainty grew to be too much. He rolls out of bed and yanks his shirt over his head, revealing the hard planes and rugged valleys of his muscular physique. My jaw drops, and I can't help but stare.

"You need a drool rag?" he teases.

I snap my mouth shut and swing my legs to the floor. "Just taking a minute to admire the landscape."

"Well, take your shirt off so we can both take a minute together."

I stifle a laugh and grip the fabric of his borrowed shirt. Ever so slowly, I tease him with a slightly sexy but more of an awkward and gangly striptease. My bra is in the wash, which means Aiden receives an unobstructed view of my breasts the moment I pull the top over my head.

The hitch in his breath makes me smile. Pulling the shirt off, I toss it to the ground.

"Well?"

It takes everything not to cross my arms over my chest. Now is not the time for my innate shyness to make an appearance, but from the hunger in his gaze, and his open admiration, I find myself standing still. Not a single twitch. I swallow against the thickness in my throat.

He tugs at the band of his jeans. "Together?" He arches a brow and I give a slow nod.

Together, we slip out of our clothes. I wear nothing beneath mine and have to wait while he pauses in the middle of stepping out of his jeans. A pair of black briefs, tented with his arousal, keep me from seeing the rest of him. He takes a step forward, but I hold up my palm.

"Uh-uh, strip."

"If you think I'm going to wait …"

"Strip," I say, needing to level the playing field.

He gives me a wink. "Eager to see what I'm packing?"

"And more," I tease back.

He tugs at the waistband of his briefs. The head pokes out over the elastic band. In one fluid movement, he removes the briefs and steps out of them to come at me. His cock bobs free.

"I gotta feel you," he says. And he does exactly that with a gleam in his eyes.

That glint twists my insides and hitches my breathing. I try to take a breath but fail before his lips crush mine. In the next few minutes, I lose myself in the tangle of limbs that grope and explore, tease and arouse, and drive me mad with need.

He's everywhere at once, cupping my breasts, pinching my nipples, licking and sucking my neck, and his fingers move lower down, delving between my legs to drive me insane with the need for more.

While he leads, I don't stand still, taking the opportunity to acquaint myself with the dips and valleys of the muscles girding his frame. As he slips a finger inside my pussy, I grab his shaft.

"Fuuuck …" His low groan encourages me to squeeze and stroke, and I lift on tiptoe as he slips another finger inside of me and curls both fingers until he hits that spot.

"Aiden …" My grip tightens on his hard length, and I lean my head against his shoulder.

"Goddamn, but you're exquisite." His voice comes in a low growl, vibrating deep in his chest. With a look, he rocks his hips into my hand, unabashedly showing me his need, and mirrors that movement with his fingers, which pump inside of my core.

I claw at his shoulders. This is easily the most erotic, and sublime, experience of my life. The awkwardness I've always known with others never enters the equation. I feel uninhibited, free to explore and feel, knowing Aiden doesn't place any judgment on what happens between us.

With him, my body comes alive. I simply feel, and I don't think, or worry, or obsess about anything. He takes all decisions away from me, guiding us onto the bed while sucking and nipping at my hard nipples. His fingers, perfectly slanted to stroke my core, keep up their maddening glide.

I'm on my back by the time his lips find mine once more. And then, the world drifts away as our bodies glide against each other.

"I can't wait to sink inside of you." He growls against my lips.

I suck in a deep breath as he moves me the way he wants. My

core clenches and trembles with wanton lust as his hands position my legs, my hips, and even my arms. After he's satisfied, the tiny rip of a foil packet barely stops the rhythm of our bodies. He sheathes himself and then aligns with my aching body. Staring down at me, his mesmerizing gaze holds me fast.

"You're amazing." With those words, he rocks forward, stretching me in one painful yet pleasurable thrust. "Don't think I intend to be gentle. I'm going to fuck you the way you deserve to be fucked. Raw. Hard. Unapologetic. You deserve nothing less than a brutal, soul-cleaving, fuck."

My whimper escapes into the small room, bouncing off the wall as he shifts his weight and braces himself. I wrap my hands around his neck and hang on for dear life.

"Oh God! Yes, Aiden! Please." I bite at my lip as he moves. With his neck bent, his forehead brushes against mine as he coaxes another moan from my lips.

"Don't keep it in, luv. There's no one near who can hear. I want to hear you scream. I want to hear my name on your lips." He kisses me, taking my moans into him, and rocks.

He's right. Soft and gentle isn't how this should go. I need to be taken and claimed, not pampered and treated with kid gloves. My core clenches around him, and I wrap my legs around his hips with a ferocity that surprises me. Then his hips flex and he drives into me, releasing the animal inside as he chases our pleasure.

My skin draws taut. My entire body clenches. I scream as heat builds within me, growing larger and more powerful with each excruciating thrust. I'm not sure how much harder he can thrust, but Aiden finds a way, pounding into me while I scream his name.

He sets a demanding pace, the delicious glide in and out generates the most amazing sensations, and his eyes, blown black with lust, respond with an unstoppable need.

I try to muffle my cries, but something inside lets loose. A spark flares, and the inferno ignites. The whole world seems to explode and splinters into a million pieces as my entire body detonates around his in pure ecstasy.

I float in Aiden's embrace, lost in the woodsy scent of him and the combined aroma of our passion, as he chases his release. With a grunt, his body jerks as he pumps inside of me until he collapses with a satisfied moan. With my head on the pillow, I wrap my arms around his neck and nuzzle his tender skin.

"That was amazing," I say, laying a line of kisses from his jaw to his collarbone.

"We're not done yet."

"We're not?"

"Have you reached your limit?" He touches my lips as passion flickers in my eyes. "Because I haven't. Not even close."

With that, my heart flutters and soars in infinite possibilities. I don't worry about what he might do. I trust him completely, but can I take any more?

I will soon find out.

Chapter Sixteen

Ariel

WITH MY ENTIRE WORLD BLISSFULLY SHATTERED, I STARE INTO THE most amazing blue eyes. That's when I feel it.

The calm.

The absence of sound.

"Aiden?"

He leans down and nuzzles my neck. "What hun?"

"Do you feel it? Or rather not feel it? It's so quiet." I drag my hand up his arm and cock my head, listening.

He glances up. I look out the window and see a brilliant blue sky.

"Get up!" I slap at his arm. "Get up! Get up! Get up!"

"Wow, I can honestly say I've never been pushed out of bed so fast after an epically good fuck. No round two?"

"As much as I'd love a round two, look!" I point. "We're in the eye! Aiden, we're in the eye. I want to see it. Please," I beg, "let's go outside."

He rolls out of bed and shoves his feet into his trousers. I follow, choosing to put on my flight suit rather than his clothes. It makes more sense, even if I regret no longer being covered in his things.

"We have to find the others." I rush to dress and shove my feet into my boots. "How many people have actually been in the eye of a hurricane?"

"Give me a second, luv. I'm two steps behind you." He zips his heavy work boots and gestures to the door. "Let's round up the troops."

I bounce with excitement and head down to sickbay. Popping my head in, I find Andrew sleeping in one of the gurneys beside his patients.

"Andrew," I call out. "We're in the eye."

His lids slide open. "Really?"

"Yeah. Aiden and I are going outside."

"We can do that?"

Aiden gives a nod. "At least until the eyewall hits."

Randall turns over and stretches. "Actually, it's probably a good idea. We can do a quick recon and see if there's any damage."

A few minutes later, Aiden, Randall, and Duncan help me and my team into brightly colored orange jumpsuits, outside gear Aiden calls it, and fits us with safety harnesses. We leave Jeffery and Caleb in the sickbay after Andrew pronounces them stable.

Jeffery is alert, in pain, but conscious. Caleb wakes intermittently, according to Andrew, with longer periods of lucidness, which he says is a good thing.

Heading outside into the eye is a nearly spiritual event.

"Wow," I say, barely breathing in reverence for the epic phenomenon. "I mean, you read about it, but this is incredible."

The sky is clear above us. The winds are light, practically nonexistent. It's as if the entire world pauses to catch its breath.

And there are birds.

"Aiden, look." I point to a handful of seabirds circling overhead. "Do you think they'll be okay?"

"I've heard of that before. The eye can be several miles across; as long as they stay in the eye, they should be fine." He takes in a deep breath. "It's profound, and eerie how calm it is, but the eyewall will be here soon enough." He points to his men. "We're going to do a quick recon of the rig and will be back. The three of you stay put."

"Don't you want us with you?" I want to see the rig.

"We'll be pushing it as it is, and I don't need to be distracted by people who aren't intimately familiar with the rig."

I try not to be too upset but understand his reasons.

"No problem," Larry says. "We'll be good little guests and just hang here. It's stunning."

"Good." Aiden heads away with Randall and Duncan in tow.

Larry turns to me as I watch Aiden walk away. "Any idea how long we have?"

I don't like being separated from Aiden and hope he and his men don't stay out too long. The rig's a big place, although the three men probably know every nook and crevice.

"I'm not sure about Julian's eye, but from the speed it was tracking earlier, I'd say no more than thirty minutes, probably less," I say.

"Wow, and then what?" Andrew's brows climb his forehead.

"Instant storm," I say. "The eyewall is the fiercest part of a hurricane. We're going to go from eerie calm to destructive winds in minutes."

"I'm not looking forward to more of that," Andrew says. "All night long, the groaning of the rig kept me up, and the pounding of the waves had me freaking out. I just kept thinking the rig was going to tip over."

"No kidding." Larry tilts his face to the sky. "Are we going to see the wall before it hits? Or does it come in gradually?"

"From what I've heard, it's a literal wall. Things will kick up a bit, but then the fiercest part of the storm will hit us. It's one massive tower of thunderstorms of epic proportions." I brace my hands on my hips and soak in the beauty of a once-in-a-lifetime event.

"Shame we can't take off and fly out," Larry says.

"No kidding, but the helicopter can't fly that high." He turns to me. "Can it?"

"Sorry, those clouds are well above our ceiling. Not enough air that high for the blades to bite into. We're grounded until this passes over."

"Well, let's hope the rig doesn't tip over."

"How about we not talk about the rig falling over"? I place my hand over my eyes and peer up into a crystal blue sky. "This is amazing." I spin in a circle, taking it all in, and my eyes catch on the helideck. "Hey guys, how about we check out the helicopter?"

"Aiden said to stay put," Andrew says with a sniff.

"He said," I counter, "that we shouldn't wander around the rig. The helideck isn't technically the rig, and what if the helicopter was damaged during the storm, or the stays came loose?"

"She has a point," Larry agrees.

"I don't know. What if you get caught when that eyewall hits?" Andrew asks.

"We're just going to go look," I counter.

"And if there's damage? What exactly are you going to do? It's not like you're going to fix anything," Andrew argues.

"Then why did Aiden go out?" I ask.

"How the hell should I know? It's a fucking oil rig. Maybe they can fix shit that's broken."

"In twenty minutes?" I nibble at my lower lip, suddenly worried for Aiden.

Andrew has a point. If we find damage, there isn't a lot of time to do anything about it. If we try and lose track of time, we could get caught out on the rig without shelter.

"Maybe we should go after them?" I ask.

"We don't even know where they are." Larry peers out in the direction Aiden and the others went. "Don't worry, Ariel, I'm sure they'll be fine."

"Fine?" That's a shit word, something people say right before the shit hits the proverbial fan. "I just want to check on the helicopter. Don't make me go alone."

Andrew and Larry exchange looks, then agree to check out the helicopter. I think they're restless, like me, and need an escape from the crew facilities. This place might be built to withstand hurricanes and tropical storms, but it feels like a prison bunker inside. I don't know how Aiden handles it.

We move quickly, mindful of safety protocols. One hand on a railing at all times. As we traverse the catwalk connecting us to the helideck, I take time to admire the churning of the ocean two hundred feet below.

Calm might be the operative word, but the ocean still feels the power of the storm. Then I remember what Aiden said about giant waves and give a shudder. What will happen if a hundred-foot wave hits the rig?

We make a quick inspection of the helicopter. All the clamps hold the skids in place and the tension wires securing the blades remain tight. There's nothing loose. Everything is buttoned down in preparation for the storm, but we make a circuit of the deck just in case.

When we return to the crew quarters, I stop short at a very angry and red-faced Aiden.

"You were told to stay put." His voice vibrates with barely suppressed fury.

"I just wanted to check on the helicopter."

The wind blows a stray strand of hair against my cheek and into my eye. I blink against the tiny sting, then notice the birds are gone, and the light fades to a pale gray, which overshadows the bright blue from moments before. I look to the south and gasp at a towering wall of clouds in the distance.

I've seen hundreds of thunderstorms, flown around their towering clouds while watching lightning dance within their stormy depths, but I've never seen a menacing wall of superstorms barreling down on me.

"Look." I point south. "It's coming."

"Yes," Aiden says. "It's coming, and you were out gallivanting around an oil rig you had no business screwing around on. Everyone. Inside. Now!" When the others file in, Aiden grabs my arm, holding me back. "Don't you ever do something as foolish as that again."

"It was nothing."

His grip tightens. "It was everything. Your safety is my responsibility. I know you're used to being in charge, doing whatever the hell you please, but on my rig, I'm the boss, and you will respect my authority."

"Aiden ..." His anger takes me by surprise, even if he has every right to be furious with my actions. "I'm sorry. I didn't think—"

"Damn straight, you didn't think."

"Look, I apologize. You're right. What I did was irresponsible and disrespectful of your authority. It won't happen again."

"Damn straight, it won't. I can't do anything to Andrew and Larry, they're your men, and they follow your lead, but shit Ariel ..." He runs his hand through my hair as the first, fat drops of rain begin to fall. "Don't you ever scare me like that again."

I gulp and my insides clench with shame. Everything between us was going well, and I fucked things up.

I place a hand on his arm. "I really am sorry."

"Not as sorry as you're going to be when you're over my knee and your ass is cherry red."

"Aiden?"

He rolls his eyes and pulls at his face. "It's what you deserve, but honestly, I'm too angry right now. Just get inside. I have a feeling the second half of this storm is going to be a rough ride."

Chapter Seventeen

Aiden

I CAN'T BELIEVE ARIEL'S CAVALIER ATTITUDE. AFTER ALL OF MY warnings and safety talks, she ignored me and went off half-cocked. Anything could have happened to her and her men during their very dangerous walkabout.

Up to the helideck? Is she crazy?

The worst thing about it is Ariel thinks nothing of it, ignorant about the inherent dangers of everything onboard a rig.

Over my knee is exactly where she belongs, but we've yet to explore any of that. We've known each other for less than a day, and I seethe over the arrogance of her actions. I might be into a little kink here and there, but I'll never strike a woman in anger.

For pleasure, I'll do any number of mutually consenting activities, but I'll never raise a hand while anger boils in my blood. It's best to join the others and ride out the second half of Julian's rage while I calm down.

The wind kicks up, roaring once again with fury. Weird that it was crystal blue moments ago. Dark gray covers the sky and blots out the sun. The rain returns, not in sprinkles but in blanketing sheets. I follow Ariel inside and seal us in as I lock the door.

We're only halfway through this damn storm.

Back in sickbay, I spend a few moments talking with Jeffery about his legs, asking about the pain. Caleb is awake and sitting up. The flight nurse, Andrew, thinks Caleb suffers nothing more than a concussion but still can't rule out a bleed in his head. There's nothing to do but observe him and give Tylenol for the pain.

I do what I can to lift their spirits and plan for worst-case scenarios in my mind. My motto is plan for the worst, brace for the best. That way, I'll never be surprised or caught unprepared.

An uncomfortable tension hangs between me and Ariel.

I keep my distance, afraid I'll snap at her in front of the others and say something inappropriate. From the way she keeps a wide berth, she definitely senses my lingering anger. My gaze constantly darts to her.

When I catch her staring, she quickly looks away. Gathered with the others around a gurney turned poker table, I'm surprised to see her holding her ground against the others.

Caleb drifts off, complaining of a headache, and Jeffery's face draws tight with pain. Jeffery tries to shrug it off, but it's clear he isn't handling things well.

I go to Andrew and whisper in his ear. Andrew gives a nod and leaves the poker game to give Jeffery something stronger than Tylenol. I slip into Andrew's place at the game, placing myself directly opposite Ariel. She refuses to make eye contact.

"What's the buy-in?" I ask.

Larry snorts and tosses me a mixed stack of Band-Aids, alcohol wipes, and 2x2 bandages.

"What's with this shit anyway?" I separate the odd assortment of chips and search Larry's face for an explanation.

"I'm a recovering gambler," Larry says. "I don't bet with money."

"If you're a recovering gambler, doesn't that mean no gambling at all?"

"It's not like alcoholics anonymous. I can get my fix, just not with actual cash." He points to the odd assortment in front of me. "Alcohol pad is a buck. Band-Aids are a five-piece, and 2x2s are ten bucks a pop."

"And here I was expecting pennies. Okay, deal me in."

The rig groans and shakes with powerful winds as the eyewall slams into us. For a moment, it feels as if the whole place shifts.

Duncan and I exchange a look. We've discussed nearly every eventuality on our short exploration of the rig. Despite the ferocity Julian leveled at us, we haven't come upon any significant damage.

The poker game continues. My stack of bandages, Band-Aids, and alcohol pads dwindles while Larry's pile increases. I glance at Ariel's stack, impressed by the number of 2x2s she manages to hang on to. We still haven't said a word to each other.

The monotony of card playing takes the edge off my anger, and I force myself to see things from her point of view. That doesn't mean I agree with her, and we will have a private conversation later, but I know her heart was in the right place.

"Did you feel that?" Larry puts his cards down. "I don't remember it shaking like this before."

"That's just waves hitting the supports," Duncan says.

"If you say so." Larry doesn't look convinced.

Ariel asks for a card and tosses a Band-Aid on the pile. Her eyes flick up to me, and while I try to catch and hold onto her warm brown eyes, her gaze flitters to the side and back to her cards.

I fold. "I'm out." With one Band-Aid and two alcohol pads left to my name, I'm done with this game. "I'm going to the Control Room to check on the progress of the storm."

"How much longer do you think?" Randall, who has been mostly quiet while he reads his book in the corner of the room, looks up.

"Half a day?" Those are the first words out of Ariel's mouth since I locked everyone inside.

"Ugh." Randall puts his book down.

"You might want to get some shut-eye," I suggest. "We're still doing twelve-hour shifts until we're done with this." I push off and head to the door. I'm surprised to see Ariel join me. "You don't have to come."

"What about the buddy system?" she asks, pulling back with uncertainty.

"I don't need a buddy," I snap. "Go ahead and stay with the others. I'll be back in a bit."

Her expression hardens, and she follows me out into the hall. Pulling the door shut, she crosses her arms beneath her breasts and stares me down.

"Did I do something wrong?"

"Do you need to ask?" I tamp down my anger. Yelling serves no purpose.

"If it's about going to the helideck, I needed to check on the helicopter."

I spin her against the wall and bracket her in, bracing my palms against the wall. "And what would you have done? There was no time to do anything, fix anything. It was reckless and dangerous. When I tell you to do something, you do it."

Her wide, surprised, eyes take me in. "Why are you making such a big deal out of this?"

"A big deal?" I close my eyes and take a calming breath. "You don't get it, do you?"

"I don't. Why are you angry?"

"Hun, you don't understand how dangerous this place can be, and that's on a good day. Anything can happen, and it only takes a moment of distraction for disaster." I point back to the sickbay. "That's what happened with Jeffery and Caleb, and they're experienced with our safety protocols. One second of not paying attention," my voice rises with the resurgence of my anger, "and now, Jeffery's legs are smashed. Caleb has a concussion. And because of that, all of us are now stuck on a rig in the middle of a damn hurricane. One mistake. That's all it takes."

"I didn't think—"

"No, you didn't. You didn't think it would be a problem. You decided that, despite my orders to stay put, but that's not why I'm upset."

She grips my shirt. "Then why?"

"Other than the fact you had no idea what you'd find on the way to the helideck, or on it, I'm pissed because you didn't trust me. You didn't respect my decision or my right to make it."

"That's not true."

"Isn't it?" Her doe-eyed stare tells me everything I need to know. It's time to establish a hard truth.

"I trust you, Aiden. I have nothing but the utmost respect for you."

I drop my hands from the wall and take a step back, and then another until I back against the opposite wall. I cross my arms. "Look, things between us are a little complicated—"

"Complicated?" Her brows lift. "That's a word people use when they're calling things off." A look of disgust ripples across her angelic features. "I thought you were different." She pivots and takes a step back toward sickbay.

"Be very careful about the next words out of your mouth," I say, "because I can damn sure guarantee you that you're one hundred percent wrong with what's going on in that head of yours."

She turns back to me, head canted to the side. I can see thoughts churning in her head. Pain lingers there. Betrayal. Fear, too. If she thinks I'm going to bail on her after a single disagreement, then she's in for a surprise.

Her lips press into a thin line, and I can see the effort she puts into not blurting out what she wants to say.

I lift a knee and kick my ankle back to brace against the wall. "Let me uncomplicate things for you. On this rig, I'm boss. That means you obey every order I give. If I tell you to jump, you ask me how high. What you don't do is take my orders as suggestions, because they aren't. That's non-negotiable. I know you wanted to check on the helicopter, but I also know the storm could have kicked up any number of hazards. There could have been debris up there, or the helicopter could have shifted. Duncan, Randall, and I needed to check on the rig and make sure the cap on the drill rig is secure. This is a part of our safety protocols. What I didn't need was to worry about what you're up to."

She opens her mouth, but I stop her with a raised hand.

"You don't get to speak yet. Not until I'm done. What I expect is for you to respect my position. If any of my men had gone against a direct order, I would have taken them off shift and shipped them off the rig permanently. I don't allow disobedience among my crew. I can't afford it, but that's not why I'm upset with you."

"It's not?"

"Not by a long shot. And as for complicating things between us? I'm not going anywhere."

"What does that mean?" Her hand lifts to press against her belly.

"I'll never interfere in your professional life. I respect you and the job you do, but between us, I take the lead. I'm upset with you because I told you to stay put and you didn't. You disregarded my wishes." I run a hand through my hair, worried this will be a deal-breaker for her, but hopeful my instincts aren't wrong.

"Aiden," she says, "I'm sorry."

"I don't need to be worried about your safety out there." My gut clenches thinking about all the things that could've happened to her. "It distracts me knowing you were climbing about the helideck when I know it's unsafe. Being distracted is dangerous. I'm not always going to be able to explain every decision I make. I'll always consider your wishes first, and include you, taking into consideration your needs. Know every decision I make about us will always be in our best interest, yours as well as mine. If we're going to continue, that's a truth you need to accept."

"Aiden ..."

"I'm not done, and please don't interrupt me."

She gives a tight nod.

"I'm upset because you were reckless with your safety, and you had no consideration as to how that would affect me."

Her lips part as my words sink in, and she drops her gaze, "I'm sorry. That's not what—"

"Not what you intended?"

Her gaze bounces up to meet my stare, then skitters sideways.

"That's the problem, Ariel."

I kick off from the wall and come to her, placing my hands on her shoulders. Dipping down to get eye-to-eye with her, I soften my tone. My anger is gone, and in its place, a fierce protectiveness takes over.

"Look, I don't know what other men have done to you. I don't know why you believe I would fuck you and walk away. You're going to tell me all about it someday, but you need to understand one thing."

Her eyes shimmer with tears.

I wipe at her cheek. "I'm not going anywhere, but if you want to continue this … if you decide you want to explore what's going on between us, then we need to come to an understanding."

"I thought …"

"I know what you thought, but do you understand what I'm saying?"

"I do."

"Good. Take time to think about it, and when you're ready, you let me know. The ball's in your court. I won't force you to do anything, or agree to anything you don't want, but what happened out there …" I make a vague gesture down the hall and the sealed door leading outside. "That can never happen again."

"I got it."

"Good. Why don't you head back to the others and think about what I said?"

"I'd rather come with you." Her lips curve up then slide back down with a tremble.

"No. I think we need a moment apart and time for you to think about what it is you want." I kiss her forehead and spin her back around, facing the sickbay. "I'll be back in a minute."

Chapter Eighteen

Ariel

A MINUTE STRETCHES TO TEN MINUTES, THEN TO THIRTY. AFTER AN hour, my nerves are fried. Aiden's words echo in my mind, swirling with all kinds of emotion I don't understand.

Do I want to continue whatever this crazy, unstoppable thing is between us? Am I interested in the other things he offers?

Most definitely, and resoundingly, that answer comes back as an unequivocal yes.

Can I do that according to his terms?

That answer is a much more tentative yes, but it is still a yes. I don't understand everything but grasp the basics. He wants control, not absolute control, but something which speaks to primal instinct. He doesn't hide what he wants, and I respect that.

Truth is, I'm not afraid to yield to him, especially knowing he will always consider my needs first, but to concede that control terrifies me as much as it excites me. It feels deliciously wonderful.

A buzzing sensation runs rampant through my body. Memories of his touch and what we did together make me wish for more; more of his touch but also more of his dominant presence. I spent a career dealing with dominant assholes but find nothing repulsive about Aiden's dominant tendencies. Quite the opposite.

It turns me on.

Initially, I thought he went over the top with his anger, but once I realize the source of it, my heart blooms. It has nothing to do with disobeying, although that's a part of it. He's angry because I placed myself at risk.

He cares for me. Not that he comes right out and admits it, but I triggered his fear by placing myself at risk. Nobody ever cared that much about me—ever.

He says he won't interfere in my career, but he has to understand the risks inherent to being a pilot. Aiden is a smart man. I'm sure he understands. He can't keep me from danger. If he can separate himself from that, then can I give him the rest?

Probably.

For the hundredth time, I glance at the door and stamp down any thoughts of going in search of him. Although he violates his rule, he's been clear about the use of the buddy system for me and my crew.

Maybe I can get Duncan to take me to the Control Room?

A glance at the seriousness of Duncan's expression as he regards his cards and I discard that notion. Randall is no help. He left to catch some shut-eye. Andrew departs as well, headed to whatever bunk was assigned to him for the duration of our stay.

For the moment, I'm stuck, which gives me plenty of time to think about what I want.

Meanwhile, Julian roars outside. Waves beat at the support legs of the rig, sending shockwaves vibrating through the steel superstructure.

The eyewall slams into us with ten times the fury of the first half of the storm. Not unexpected, it's ass-puckering. Things should get better from here on out, but how much longer will we have to stay? How much longer will Aiden leave me alone?

Another powerful shudder rips through the rig. I glance at Larry, and his gaze meets mine, but he doesn't seem concerned. He counts out three Band-Aids and lays them down on the gurney. Duncan places his bet and picks up another card. I spin around, looking again at the door, but still no Aiden. With a huff, I stand, stretch, and go to the gurney to join the guys.

"Deal me in," I say. "I'm going stir crazy."

Larry counts out an assortment of Band-Aids, alcohol wipes, and 2x2 bandages. He deals me in with the next round. An hour later, and still, there's no Aiden.

Larry glances up. "I'm sure he'll be back soon."

"Is it that obvious?"

"You want an honest answer, or should I lie?" Larry folds, leaving me and Duncan in the game.

"Lie."

"It's not obvious," Larry says.

Duncan snorts.

"Hit me." I grab the card dealt by Larry and look at my hand. It's shit, but Duncan doesn't know that. Three 2x2s land in the betting pile. "Raise you."

Duncan arches a brow. "Interesting." He takes a long hard look at me, but I reveal nothing. With a huff, he tosses his cards on the table.

I scoop up the pot and add it to my stack.

"Aren't you going to show me your cards?"

"Nope," I say with a grin.

"Aw shit, did you just take me?"

"Maybe, maybe not," I tease.

"I don't know if you're fucking with me or not."

I don't answer.

The deck-plating beneath our feet rumbles and Larry groans. "I'm getting really tired of that."

The door to the sickbay opens and Aiden looks in. "Duncan, a word ..." His tight expression flicks to me and he tries to soften it with a smile. It doesn't work. Something is up. I start to get up, but Aiden shakes his head. "Just Duncan. We'll be back in a bit."

Duncan leaves with Aiden. I toss my cards on the gurney.

Larry gives a snicker. "You little shit. You had nothing."

"Not a thing." I reach for the cards Duncan left and flip them over. "Two pair."

Larry and I laugh as he deals out a hand of gin rummy. Before long, I realize Aiden and Duncan have yet to return.

"You think we should go find them?"

Larry picks up a card. "And where would we begin looking?"

"I don't know, but they've been gone awhile."

"Hmm, hasn't been that long."

"Feels like it has."

"Soooo …" Larry draws out the word, "about Aiden?"

"What about him?"

"What exactly is going on between you two? Is this serious or just a fling?"

"Why the sudden interest in my love life?"

"I don't need the gory details, but you don't date. I can count on my pinky finger the number of times you've been on a date since we met. Now, you're nearly inseparable from this guy. I need to know how thorough of a background check I need to do when we get home."

"Background check?"

"Yeah, obviously we're going to check him out."

"We?"

"Yes, your friends actually care about you. So, how thorough?"

I nibble at my lower lip.

"That bad, huh?"

"I guess so. Is it weird? I've known him for barely a day."

"And yet, he's stolen your heart."

Aiden did more than that. I give Larry a long hard look, surprised by his protectiveness, but thankful for it also.

"You might want to be thorough." And with that, my answer to Aiden's demand can't be more clear. If he'll take care of me, then I'll trust my heart to him, and everything that comes with it. Larry and I play gin rummy while we wait for Aiden.

But there is no Aiden.

After another hour, I put down my cards. "Sorry, but I'm carded out."

I go to check on our patients. Jeffery sleeps soundly, his face eased of pain. Caleb snores softly. I shake him awake and force him to sit while Larry asks him a series of questions and shines a light in his eyes.

Caleb groans. "I'm fucking tired. Let me sleep."

"Stop it," Larry says. "You know this is for the best."

Caleb rolls his eyes and lays back down.

I tug Larry aside. "If something goes wrong, it's not like we can do anything."

"Not much, but Andrew has a few tricks up his sleeve, temporizing measures until we can get him out." Larry looks to the door leading out into the hall. "It's been a few hours. I wonder how much of this storm is left?"

"It depends. Some hurricanes pass in hours; others can take a day or two."

"Well, we've already spent a day locked up," Larry says.

"As soon as the winds die down, we can take off." My gut twists at that comment. Taking off means leaving Aiden behind. And then what?

What will happen next?

"Thank fuck for that." Larry sits back on the gurney and gathers the cards, laying out a row for solitaire.

Chapter Nineteen

Aiden

THE NEWS ISN'T GOOD.

I've been with Duncan and Randall for the past couple of hours going over scenarios and contingency plans.

"Guys, bottom line, the starboard pylon is unstable."

The shifting of the rig, and the force of mammoth-sized waves slamming into it, only destabilizes it more.

"Maybe we can still ride it out." Duncan rubs at the stubble on his jaw.

"How much longer is this thing over us?" Randall glances up.

"It's a shitstorm and huge. Julian isn't done with us yet." I look to my men.

Their opinions matter, and I respect their years of experience. I hope one of them finds a solution I haven't considered because my assessment of our situation says we're in the middle of a shitstorm that is only going to get worse.

"Okay, worst-case scenario?" I poll their thoughts. "We need solutions."

"Worst case, the rig capsizes." Duncan glances at Randall, who gives a tight-lipped nod. "Best case, the skies clear, the seas calm, and we laugh about this over beers."

"Preferably on solid ground," Randall adds.

Another jarring vibration reverberates through the superstructure, and the floor beneath me rocks.

"She's not going to capsize, is she?" Duncan pulls a face.

"I hope not." I remain calm, despite the danger we face and the decisions I need to make. "At least we capped off the well. If that does happen, we won't be responsible for the worst ecological disaster of our lifetimes."

"I thought you were crazy making us do that, but I'm glad for it now." Randall heaves a weighted sigh. "So, what's the plan, boss?"

"We plan for contingencies. If Ariel can't fly the injured out, we need to figure out how to get them to the lifeboats."

"That's damn near impossible." Randall's jaw twitches.

Duncan grabs at the counter. "We'll figure out a way."

Bright red, torpedo-shaped boats, they're designed for emergency evacuation by able-bodied men. Getting a man strapped to a stretcher inside the lifeboat is more complicated, maybe impossible, and that doesn't begin to touch on how we might secure Jeffery for the drop into the seething waters below, or the hours he'll be tossed around like a cork. There is no way Jeffery can endure such torture.

"Let's hope we can avoid it." I scrub at my hair and curse. Julian is turning out to be a mean bastard. Operations will be shut down for months as we repair the damage to the rig. "Let's get ready."

"You trust the pilot?"

"I have every faith in her skills. She's flown under worse conditions than this, and she's been very upfront about her abilities. I don't think she'd bullshit us about what she can do."

"Let's say she does decide to take off," Duncan says, "that still leaves the three of us. We may still wind up puking our brains out in one of those death rafts."

"Unless something unthinkable happens, I'm not convinced we need to abandon the rig. She will ride out this storm."

"I'm glad you have faith." Randall doesn't look convinced as another shudder wracks the superstructure. "And Duncan, please don't call them death rafts."

"One way or another, a decision needs to be made. Once Ariel lets me know what she can and can't do, I'll decide our next step." The final decision falls solely on my shoulders. "Let's bring her in on this."

I head to sickbay and open the door. My gaze lands on Ariel.

"I need you in the Control Room."

"Me?" She and Larry are playing cards.

"Both of you." I point to her and Larry.

"I can't leave them." Larry looks to Jeffery and Caleb.

"Is Caleb mobile?" Aiden asks.

"Depends on what your definition of mobile is," Larry answers.

"Can he walk?"

"Yeah, I guess. He might be a bit unsteady. I wouldn't ask him to go for a jog."

"I don't need him to run." I press my lips together and my expression turns serious. "The Control Room, now." I hold the door open, waiting for Ariel and Larry to join me.

With a glance to Larry, Ariel bites at her lip and heads into the hall where Duncan waits for us. When he sees her, he pivots and heads down the hall. She follows while Larry and I pick up the rear.

When we get to the Control Room, Andrew is there. Randall yanked him out of his bunk. Andrew wipes the sleep from his eyes and yawns.

"Aiden?" Ariel turns to me. "What's going on?"

"That all depends on you."

"What do you mean?"

"What is the maximum wind speed you can take off in?"

"Forty knots is the recommended limit."

"I get that, but what can you safely take off in?"

"You're scaring me."

"Answer the question."

"Fifty or fifty-five is probably the highest."

I glance at the weather readout, then turn to Duncan. "It's

going to be tight. How long do you figure to get everyone on board?"

Duncan twists his lips. "It's not going to be easy. Can Caleb walk?"

"They say he can, but he'll need assistance."

"Okay, we've got plenty of that," Duncan replies. "Randall can help Caleb while you and I take Jeffery in the stretcher."

"Aiden …" Ariel's voice sharpens. "What the ever-loving fuck is going on? Why are we talking about evacuation now?" She points to the wind speed readout. "Those winds are too high to take off."

"I know; we'll wait as long as we can."

"Answer the question," she insists. "What's going on?"

Duncan and Randall exchange somber looks. Finally, I answer. "The rig's destabilized. The new vibrations you're feeling beneath your feet are from the starboard support leg shifting on the seabed."

"What?"

"Between the storm and the waves, we've lost our footing beneath the starboard pylon. It's only going to get worse. Fortunately, we have a little time, but we need to evacuate."

"Evacuate? They won't send a helicopter out for you. Julian is between us and the coast. They're getting slammed right now, and there's no way …"

I watch the play of emotions as they hit her face: concern, worry, comprehension, and then terror.

She staggers back. "You can't be serious? You can't get in one of those in this."

Considered unsinkable, the lifeboats launch from the height of the rig, plummeting two hundred feet into the ocean below.

"It's the only way, but we may not even have to use one. I want my injured, and you and your crew, off the rig before that becomes our only solution."

"But that's crazy," she argues.

"It's not up for negotiation. The rig is destabilized, and it's getting worse."

"What do you mean worse?"

"We don't have much time."

She glances at the prevailing wind speed and gusts. I understand the insanity behind attempting a takeoff. Not that it can't be done. I know Ariel's flown in much worse conditions but don't know if she's pushed numbers like this before. There are any number of things that can go wrong. Not to mention …

"Aiden …"

"Yes?"

"If I take off with winds that high, I can't take anyone else in the helicopter. I'll need all the lift I can get and the extra weight …"

"Don't worry, luv. We already know."

She runs a hand through her hair and swallows hard.

I grip her hands in mine. "I need to know absolute limits of what you can and can't do because I need to make a decision. The timing is going to be tight."

"Okay, maximum winds I can take off in are fifty, but any gusts over sixty, and I'm grounded." She doesn't flinch in giving her answer. Tough as nails, his girl's faced worse danger than this. Her confidence astounds me, and I love that about her the most.

"And how long to spin up?" I calculate timelines in my head, knowing how long it takes to get to the lifeboats from the helideck.

Once she takes off, my men and I will have limited time to make a decision. Escape in the lifeboats will happen only if absolutely necessary. It's safer for us to stay on the rig for as long as possible. Hopefully, the storm will pass over, and it won't be an issue. As Duncan says, we'll laugh about this over beers, somewhere on solid ground.

"Not long," she says. "I can do my pre-flights while Andrew and Larry secure our patients. Spinning up isn't the limiting factor. It's loading." Ariel turns to her crewmen for confirmation.

I play through all the variations in my head. Am I making a mistake pushing for the helicopter to take flight? Images of trying to maneuver the stretcher through the narrow opening of the lifeboat firm my resolve. The idea of being separated from Ariel, however, doesn't sit well with my gut.

Andrew leans against a counter and suppresses a yawn. "Caleb is easy. Jeffery is more complicated because it's a matter of loading and securing the stretcher. Fortunately, they're both fairly stable. I'm more concerned about getting them to the helicopter."

"We've got that covered," Randall says. "Don't worry about that. You get yourselves to the helicopter, and we'll take care of the rest."

"Do you?" Ariel pipes in. "Because it seems dangerous trying to carry a stretcher in the middle of a hurricane."

"Luv, it has to be done. It's either to the helideck or the lifeboats. I don't know about you, but I'd rather have you in the air than in one of those. As long as you say it's okay to fly, we're taking that option."

Her tiny fists clench. "What are the chances of waiting out the storm?"

"I've spent the last two hours trying to convince myself I'm wrong. I can't risk it. We're evacuating."

"You mean you're evacuating my crew and your injured men. I know you plan on staying."

"Hun, the three of us will ride things out. If it does come to abandoning the rig, we'll have a much better chance with just the three of us. That's not something I want to attempt with injured crew."

"I still have a problem."

"What's that?"

"I can't fly to Mobile. Julian is between us and land. There's no way I can head into that."

"Where can you fly?"

"Let me take a look."

She goes to the map of the Gulf, then glances over her shoulder, determination girding her expression. My girl is a fucking badass and hot as hell.

"What are the chances we can top off? If I had more fuel, I could fly to Pensacola. It's far enough out of Julian's path."

"It won't be feasible to top you off in these winds," I say.

"What about Texas?" Andrew asks. "Can we fly to Houston or Corpus Christi? What about Galveston?"

"Hmm," she taps the map. "If we fly due east, we'd be behind the storm. I think Florida is our best bet. If we topped off, I might make it to Tampa."

"You have the range for that?"

"No, but I can hop."

"Hop?" I scratch my head. "What does that mean?"

"The mobile drilling platforms that moved out of the storm's path. I can land on one of those, refuel, and continue on to Tampa."

"Decide what's best," I say. "Keep me updated. I'll see what drilling platforms are between here and there, and who can assist."

"I'll radio in, too," she says. "Let base know what's happening." She spins around. "I'm not happy about this."

I go to her, uncaring about the men watching, and pull her into a tight hug. "It's going to be all right."

"Promise?" A film of tears shimmers in my girl's eyes.

I tighten my grip and plant a chaste kiss on her lips. "Promise."

"And what about you? What happens to you?"

"Well, I won't lie. It's going to be one hell of a ride. If we do have to get into one of the life rafts, they're unsinkable. There's a beacon, of course. As soon as everything blows over, they'll send someone out to fish us out of the water."

"It just seems insane to go into the water ..."

"I know, but a lot of smart people have figured all this out. We'll be fine. I promise."

I hope it isn't the last promise I make.

Ariel places her hand on my arm. She understands.

Chapter Twenty

Ariel

BACK IN THE SICKBAY, I SIT WITH THE OTHERS AS AIDEN PREPS US TO move. He leads everyone through each step, like a pre-flight briefing, making sure there aren't any questions, while my gut churns and my palms slick with sweat.

What exactly does destabilized mean?

Caleb is up and walking, although a little unsteady. They strap Jeffery to the stretcher, making sure he won't tumble out. There are stairs and catwalks to navigate, but Aiden doesn't seem concerned.

His confidence is my anchor.

He and Duncan will head out to the helicopter with me and Larry, where they'll free the rotors from the cables that secure them against the winds. The clamps around the skids will be removed as well while I begin my pre-flight checklist.

Aiden and Duncan will head back to the crew quarters, where Andrew waits with Jeffery, Caleb, and Randall. The men will then begin the trek back up to the helideck.

Wind speeds are high, five knots below the maximum I'll fly in.

That doesn't bother me. It's the gusts that present the greatest danger.

I plot a course back to land, detouring to stop on a drillship that moved to avoid the storm. The crew is notified and will have everything in place to refuel the helicopter.

After loading our patients, Aiden and the rest will then return back over the catwalks to the emergency lifeboats dangling two hundred feet above the water.

Aiden runs us through everything one last time as the rig groans and shudders beneath our feet. At least I won't be taking off in the dark. There's that to be thankful for, although not much else.

"You ready?" Aiden turns to me, waiting for my okay. I'm the one who decides if the winds permit takeoff. I'm not ready but have enough determination, and faith, to see this through.

"Yes."

With one last check to my safety harness, he cups my cheeks. "You remember what I said …"

"Yes, one hand on the rail at all times and click into the safety cable on the stairs. I got it."

If only we had a few more hours together …

Duncan checks Andrew's harness then thumps him on the back. "Let's do this."

Wearing borrowed rain gear, Andrew and I follow Duncan out. Aiden takes up the rear as the four of us push through heavy sheets of rain. The others stay behind, waiting for their turn to head out to the helideck.

The entire world is gray. Gray sky. Gray clouds. Gray seething sea. And the waves are massive.

I stumble as I peer down into the seething maelstrom.

Aiden grabs my harness. "You okay?" He has to shout over the force of the wind.

"I shouldn't have looked down."

I wasn't prepared for the height of the swells slamming into the rig. They're easily forty to fifty feet in height and roll relentlessly forward, without a care for what might be in the way. The metal deck plating groans beneath my feet as the waves crash around the supports.

"Eyes straight," Aiden commands. "Don't look down." His bossy attitude doesn't bother me one bit.

I need the motivation it provides to keep me moving forward. I've flown many missions in my life, harrowing flights into and out of sandstorms. Low visibility doesn't bother me. Winds don't bother me. Storms don't scare me.

I have enough years flying medevac in the hot and humid areas around Mobile. Dodging thunderstorms is second nature, but flying into one? Or rather, out of a hurricane? It's one item not on my list of ballsy things I want to do.

I grit my teeth. Don't look down. Easy enough to say.

Out in the distance, the waves appear larger than up close, but that's merely an optical illusion.

Hand on the rail, I focus on Andrew's back as he ascends the stairs leading up to the helicopter. Aiden and Duncan are going to have to hoist the stretcher up these stairs, and I say a small prayer for divine intervention to ease their labor.

On the helideck, there's no protection from the winds. The gusts buffet me, and I brace against them with nearly every step. Aiden comes to my side and guides me to the door of the helicopter. He holds it as I climb in, then leans forward to give me a kiss.

"Everything is going to be all right."

"Just promise me you'll be safe." I need to hear his promise, knowing some things are out of his control.

He reaches into his pocket and pulls out a folded piece of paper. "Here, put this in your pocket. Promise me you won't open it until you hit land and are safe."

I take the paper, hand trembling, and shove it in a pocket.

He's going to walk away, help Duncan release the locking clamps, and remove the stabilizing cables. This might be the last time I see him, speak to him, or touch him.

My heart squeezes with a hundred horrific possibilities, but the sparkle in his eyes gives me faith. He isn't scared, and if he isn't, then I won't be either.

The door slams shut, and I realize he forgot to kiss me goodbye. The helicopter rocks on its skids, either from the movement of the rig or from the clamps being undone.

I glance out the window and catch Aiden's wave as he and Duncan return to the stairs. Placing my fingers on my lips, I blow him a kiss. Hopefully, it won't be our last.

Andrew hops on board, sliding open the back door and shutting it just as quick. He preps the back for our passengers.

Focus!

My attention returns to a task I've done a thousand times before. Pre-flight checklists become my world as I ready for flight.

A quick look at my displays confirms I'm good to go for takeoff.

The gusts are still on the high side, and the winds peg at a sustained fifty knots. Dicey doesn't begin to describe this cluster-fuck.

As I finish my pre-flight checks, the back door opens. Caleb spills inside, and the door slams shut again. Andrew settles Caleb into a bench seat, then hops outside to help the others.

Sheets of rain obscure my view, but I watch nervously as Randall and Larry struggle at the top of the stairs.

Despite the rain, their orange environment suits are easy to spot. Aiden and Duncan must be having difficulty navigating the narrow stairs.

As my heart leaps to my throat, the men manhandle the stretcher. Slowly it rises into view, canting precariously for a moment. If Jeffery wasn't securely strapped in place, he would've fallen out.

They bring the stretcher to the side door and load Jeffery inside. Andrew hops in and Larry follows with a slam of the door. That's my signal to spin up the rotors.

It's time to leave.

Aiden, Randall, and Duncan head back to the stairs. Aiden pauses at the top for one last look. He presses his fingers to his heart, his lips, then blows me a kiss.

Brass balls and nerves of steel, this is what I live for; flying at the edge of reason, but I hate leaving Aiden behind.

As I spin up the helicopter, I track the progress of the three men in bright orange weather suits as they head toward a row of red, bullet-shaped lifeboats.

The rig shudders beneath me, a long agonizing groan, and one of the men in bright orange slips and falls. I gasp as the others help him back up.

They move at a determined pace, much slower than I feel comfortable with, but Aiden emphasizes how rushing creates a distraction. Distraction leads to accidents. The last thing they need is a repeat of what happened to Jeffery.

My headphone crackles to life as Andrew patches himself in. "All clear back here. Ready for liftoff when you are."

Laser-focused on my task, I put all thoughts of the three men in orange from my mind. The winds will make this dicey, and I agree with Aiden about distractions.

The helicopter lifts off the helideck as I white-knuckle the controls. Remembering the crane and antenna from my landing, I adjust for those hazards.

A gust rocks me to the side, but I counter with my controls. Ever so slowly, the helicopter takes flight. Using my foot controls, I spin around to head away from the rig but spare one moment to trace the path of Aiden and the others.

Three orange suits scramble to a lifeboat.

"For the love of all things holy …" Static crackles over the mic as Larry's awe-filled words blat through my headset.

"Not now." I struggle to fight the winds while gaining altitude.

"Holy shit," Andrew echoes.

Hand on the stick, feet working the pedals, I fight the storm.

Then I see it.

A wave approaches the rig.

Not a forty or fifty-footer, but one of the monster waves Aiden told me about. It crests in the distance and rolls forward without a care for what, or who, is in its path.

"Did they make it to the lifeboat?" The last I saw, all three men were outside the lifeboat.

"I don't know," Larry says. "I can't see."

I spin around and search the structure. All lifeboats are attached to the rig, but I see no men.

"Oh my God." My grip tightens, and I resist the urge to go to them, to save them, but what can I do?

There's nothing to do except watch the monster wave slam into the superstructure.

My breath catches as the rig cants beneath the hundred-foot monster. Ever so slowly, it rises as the wave pushes at the supports.

The deck tilts, slanting at an unnatural angle. The whole thing rolls, pushed around like nothing more than a child's toy bobbing like a cork.

I bite back a scream as the rig capsizes.

Everything slows down. The tilting of the rig. My laser focus on the lifeboats. The sheets of rain and the lumbering wave as it moves with lethal destruction.

The whine of the rotors fills my ears. The vibrations of the engine rattle through the seat. Wind buffets me from every direction, and I struggle to stay in the air.

But I do.

I lift us away from the capsized rig as it rolls on its side and crashes into the heaving sea. As I gain altitude, the bottom drops out of my world. My heart breaks. Tears stream down my face. And I gulp against the overwhelming pain of losing someone I love.

Aiden!

A scream struggles to rip from my throat, but I tamp down my fear and swallow my pain.

There are four others who depend on me to fly them to safety. Although, Julian has other plans about that. The monster storm tosses everything in its arsenal against me as I fly us to safety.

Gusts buffet the helicopter. Lightning crashes all around.

Updrafts yank me up while downdrafts try to slam me into the water.

I fly as high as I can, giving room to recover from the gut-wrenching drops and even scarier gusts that try to flip me in the air.

The engine groans. The rotors cut through the air. I keep us on a steady path, heading towards calmer air. Seconds tick by. Minutes pile up.

This is the job I've trained for. It's one I excel at, and I won't let my crew down.

Julian rages around me. The maddening gusts and downdrafts keep me on high alert as I turn the helicopter south.

Minutes turn to an hour as I battle the storm.

I take in a deep breath, trying to settle my nerves, and swallow past my grief. Turning on my microphone, I reach out to my crew.

"How's everyone back there?" I need to hear something positive.

"We're okay," Andrew says. "Stable and secure. You're doing great, Ariel."

I'm not doing great.

I'm falling apart, but Andrew is right about my piloting.

The sheets of rain thin, then clear. The gusts fade, petering out to nothing of concern. The thick clouds overhead break apart as I clear the inner rain bands and head to the edge of the storm.

My white-knuckled grip on the stick eases, and I shake out my hand. Eyes on my instrument cluster, I watch my fuel gauge as it drops.

The flight to the drillship takes me to the bottom of my fuel reserves, but we make it. The winds lessen, and the sky brightens. I touch down on the drillship as it floats on calm seas with bright blue skies overhead.

There isn't a cloud in the sky, as if Julian never existed.

But Julian is still out there. It swallowed an oil rig and took three men with it.

The crew of the drillship top off my tanks. I'm back in the air in less than an hour and headed to Tampa with my injured still on board.

Tears spill down my cheeks, not knowing if Aiden and the others made it. The lifeboat didn't release when the wave hit. After that, I don't remember much else, too preoccupied with fighting the storm.

My heart clenches. My gut churns. I want to break down and cry, but there's still a job to be done.

And I do it.

Years of flying, and over a thousand hours in the air, help me to focus on the job. I don't allow myself to think about anything else and try not to let hope die in my heart.

The Coast Guard is notified about Aiden and his men. Those on the drillship make sure that happens, and a search will be underway as soon as possible. There's still hope.

When I land in Tampa, it's to a beautiful, sunny day. The sun sets to the west across the Gulf, sinking below the water in a blaze of yellows and reds.

Somewhere out there, Aiden struggles to survive.

Or so I hope.

Chapter Twenty-One

Ariel

AFTER A DAY SPENT WAITING FOR JULIAN TO DOWNGRADE FROM A hurricane to a tropical storm and stagger inland, where it finally gasps and fizzles into weakened bands of thunderstorms, I bring Andrew and Larry home to Mobile.

I avoid them while grounded in Tampa, heading to my hotel for the night, where I spend the entire evening crying until my eyes burn.

The flight home is a somber affair, and I mute my headset microphone so the guys can't hear my gut-wrenching cries. After dropping them off at the base, despite their protests, I wave away their offers of food and company.

Calls to the Coast Guard rip out my heart and gut me from the inside out. There is no sign of an emergency beacon assigned to any of the lifeboats on the rig.

They'll get back to me.

I'll be the first to know.

They promise, but a week later, there's still no word.

My apartment is a mess. I've been neglecting it. Hell, I've been neglecting everything.

Grease slicks in my hair, and my pits stink. I ran out of clean clothes because I can't find the motivation to wash them. When I sniff a discarded pair of panties to see if they're okay to reuse, I decide enough is enough.

First order of business, I need a shower.

With my hair washed and smelling of lilac and rose, rather than horrendous body odor, I set to the task of gathering my clothes. At the bottom of the pile, I find my discarded flight suit. Still damp, it reeks to high heaven.

Work gave me a week's time off, but it'll soon be time to get back into the pilot's seat. The only problem is all I can think about is Aiden and his baby blues.

As I load the washer, I check the pockets of my flight suit and bring out the damp remnants of Aiden's note. Cradling it in my hand, I battle a new influx of tears. It's the only thing I have from him.

With a swipe to my cheeks, I wipe away my tears. He made me promise not to read it until I got safely to land, but in the chaos of the flight, I forgot all about the note. Or maybe my mind played a trick on me?

Carefully, I unfold the paper, trying not to tear the fragile layers. The ink on the paper ran, but I can still make out the bold, determined strokes of Aiden's hand.

DEAR ARIEL,

DO NOT CRY FOR ME. DON'T WORRY. I'LL MOVE HEAVEN AND EARTH TO find you. It will take more than a hurricane to take me from the one I want, and know that I want every piece of you very much. Because of that, I will return to you. Have faith in me.

. . .

Love,
  Aiden.

GUT-WRENCHING SOBS OVERCOME ME. I DROP THE NOTE AND collapse on the floor. He's gone. I punch at the pile of dirty clothes and all the unfairness of the universe.

"You promised me! You promised!"

My cries pierce the air and bounce off the walls, ringing in my ears. I rock back and forth, tucking my knees to my chest. The ringing continues.

Ringing?

I cock my head; that sound comes from the doorbell. Wrapped in nothing more than my robe, towel tight around my wet hair, I scream at whoever has the balls to knock on my door. Don't they know my entire world is falling apart?

The last thing I need is someone trying to sell me something.

"Go away!"

My shout does nothing to dissuade the person behind the door. They revert to pounding.

"Go. The. Fuck. Away!" I toss a book at the door. It hits with a solid thunk and tumbles to the floor.

"Ariel, I swear, if you don't open this door right now, I'll put you over my knee, and you won't be able to sit for weeks. I've come a long way to see you!"

My entire body stills.

It can't be.

"Ariel!" His voice. "Open ..." His amazing ..."The Goddamn ..." Beautiful voice. "Door!"

"Aiden?" I scramble up from the floor and run to the door. Yanking it open, the most amazing blue eyes take me in.

"I hope to hell that's not how you open the door for all the guys."

I look down and gasp at my gaping robe. My boobs flash him along with everything else. Grabbing my robe, I try to cover up, but Aiden holds my wrists and steps inside.

As the door shuts, his lips crash down on mine, flooding me with warmth, and setting off an inferno inside my body.

"Aiden," I say on a sigh. "How ...? What happened?"

He shrugs my robe off my shoulders.

"They were supposed to call me with news," I say beneath his kisses.

"Ariel ..." His lips trail over my jaw and down my neck. "Shut the fuck up and show me where the bed is. I need to be inside of you. Now."

My heart swells with joy. Seeing him safe and sound is only half as good as feeling him in my arms. All the fears rattling around inside my head flit away. My grief evaporates.

Aiden is alive and looking amazing as always. His forever blue eyes welcome me into his arms, and I tumble into his heart. Right where I belong.

"You have to tell me what happened," I say. "That monster wave picked up the rig and tossed it like a toy."

"Is that what happened?"

"You didn't know? I was so worried. The three of you were outside as I was lifting off, then the wave hit. I didn't see the boat launch."

"Oh, it launched all right. Worst rollercoaster ride in the world. I don't recommend it."

Images of the wave hitting the rig bring back that horrible sinking feeling in my gut. "I thought you died."

"It's going to take more than a monster wave to keep me from you. Didn't I tell you to have a little faith?"

If faith is all it takes, I have plenty of that. Words don't form in my head as he backs me up against the bed.

"I'm going to fuck you. I'm going to bury myself so deep you'll never forget me. It's all I could think about while bobbing around like a cork." He snickers. "Well, that and not throwing up."

"You know, talk about you spewing your guts isn't very sexy."

"It's not?"

I grin as I shake my head. "No, it's not."

"Well, then let me get my sexy on."

"Get your sexy on?" I giggle. "That's even worse."

"Oh yeah, you ain't seen nothing yet." He pushes me back onto the bed and pulls his shirt over his head. Holy rippled abs. I almost forgot how magnificent he is.

I lick my lips.

"You like that?"

"Yes."

He tugs at his belt buckle. "Hmm, well, I think you're going to like this even more."

With a wiggle of his hips, he seduces me with the world's worst male striptease, but I don't care. Aiden lightens the mood and has me giggling as he strips out of his clothes.

Then he yanks my ankle and pulls me down the bed. His kisses begin at my toes, meander up my legs, have me moaning by the time he reaches my thighs, and screaming moments later as the roughness of his stubble rubs between my legs, tickling *that spot* until I come.

As I spin down from ecstasy, he's on the move again, lips leading, hands following, lighting all my nerves on fire. He takes control of my body and worships every inch of my skin. When he finally finds my lips, he positions me as he likes.

Lips touch lips. Skin slides against skin. I moan with the sudden stretch of him filling me inside. Pleasure rather than pain fuels my screams. We come together in a tangle of limbs as the sheets twist beneath us and pleasure draws us to greater and greater heights.

Sometime the next morning, he tells me about the week he spent at sea, how the responder in the lifeboat failed to activate, and how a lovely yacht captain named Brie Hamilton rescued them and called the Coast Guard to end their week at sea.

I don't care about any of that. As long as he's in my arms, the world feels right again.

We spend most of the morning touching, kissing, and reconnecting. Eventually, though, he forces me out of bed and into the shower.

"We have a lunch date," he pronounces after fucking me against the shower wall.

"Okay, but I'd rather order in." I never want to leave.

"Ah, no. We have a lunch date with two very excited women."

"Really? Two?"

"Yes, a precocious nine-year-old who wants to meet the woman who's stolen her daddy's heart and an overly curious grandmother who's dying to check out her new daughter-in-law."

"Wow, no pressure there," I say.

Aiden gathers me in his arms. "Ariel, if you haven't figured it out yet, I'm in this for the long haul. If you're going to be a part of my family, you need to meet Callie and Mary."

Part of his family?

I'm going to meet his kid? And his dead wife's mother?

Chapter Twenty-Two

Aiden

I HOLD BACK A LAUGH AT THE TERROR FILLING ARIEL'S EXPRESSION. She looks like she wants to crawl into a black hole and never come out. That doesn't dissuade me from what I plan.

I spent the worst week of my life thinking about my future.

In between puking my guts out, fighting nausea, and surviving a week adrift, I decide not to wait another minute for a second chance at happiness.

I know what I want, and I'm not willing to waste any more time chasing my dream.

Ariel feels good in my arms and fits perfectly around my cock. She brings a smile to my face and makes my heart race. The woman is my kryptonite. Now, I need to make her mine forever.

"Get dressed! We're going to be late."

Ariel gives a squeak. "You can't make me."

"I can, and I will. Now, Callie is waiting to meet you, and you don't want to keep a nine-year-old waiting. Trust me. The fallout is horrendous."

"Aiden, you're out of your mind."

"Callie is excited to meet you."

"I don't know that I can." She retreats, but I refuse to let her go.

"Have you not heard a word I've said?" I'll shout it from the rooftops. I'm head over heels in love with Ariel.

From the moment I saw her step out of that helicopter, my heart belonged to her. Some people might say it's crazy. They may be right, but then they know nothing about true love.

Callie understands. She has the wisdom of childhood and believes in a love at first sight fairy tale. I hope Ariel won't mind a few suggestions for our wedding because Callie has tons of ideas.

"You could have warned me." Ariel gives a huff, tossing her long hair over her shoulders.

I love when she lets her hair hang loose. It gives me something to grab while I fuck her from behind. My cock thickens, hungering for more. I'd take her again, except we really do need to get going.

I cross my arms over my chest. "I don't need to warn you. Now, what part of get your ass in gear do you find confusing?"

"You don't get it. I have nothing clean to wear. I smell like sex."

"Best smell in the world, at least with my scent all over you."

"I'm not meeting your daughter smelling freshly fucked."

My eyes pinch. "You know, I think we need a very special version of a swear jar."

"I won't swear in front of your kid."

"Oh, I trust you won't, but I was thinking something fun for us." I rub my palms together, heating them up.

Her gaze dips to my hands, but I don't think she understands what I mean.

"Ten." I lock stares with her, wondering if she'll figure out what I mean.

"Ten what? Ten cents or ten bucks?"

"Ten swats."

Her eyes widen, but from the way her pupils dilate and the hitching in her breathing, I struck a nerve. A very sexy and delicious nerve.

"You wouldn't?"

"I most definitely would. I love that filthy mouth of yours far too much, but the swats won't be for swearing."

She hesitates. "Then what would they be for?" Her brows pinch and a flush creeps up her neck. It colors her cheeks a rosy red.

"Simple. Disobey me and it's ten swats. How does that sound?"

Her hands cover her ass cheeks. "It sounds like I need to get dressed."

I come toward her and grip her upper arm, a soft touch meant to reassure. "I would never do anything you didn't want, but damn woman, if that's not what I want with you."

It takes a moment, but then she finally lifts her chin. Her bright eyes glitter and she holds a smile on her face.

"I'm not against it," she hesitates, "but maybe that's something that we should take slow?"

It isn't a hard no. I can deal with that, but I'll continue testing those waters until I have a definitive yes. "Understood, but we do actually have someplace to be. Callie is very eager to meet you. So, if you don't mind … I need you to get dressed."

When she drags her feet, I hurry her along. When doubt creeps across her face, I distract her with a kiss.

Eventually, I get her into the car.

A short drive later, I park at Callie's favorite restaurant and check my texts. They're already seated inside.

"You ready?" I grip Ariel's hand and give it a squeeze.

"Do I have a choice?" Her lashes flutter and she places a palm over her belly.

I can imagine her nervousness because I feel some of it too. The love of my life is getting ready to meet my kid, a daughter I treasure more than life itself. If they don't hit it off, my world will never be the same.

It's hard to convince Ariel she has nothing to fear, but she doesn't.

Although, her hesitation is understandable.

Ariel is getting ready to walk into a restaurant to meet what she thinks is the ghost of my ex-wife. That would terrify the strongest woman. What she doesn't understand is that this is exactly the future Samantha dreamed of for her husband and her daughter.

Ariel has the blessing of a woman she will never know.

"Come now," I say, trying to reassure Ariel, "you spent months in the desert getting shot at, and shot down, and you're scared of a little girl?"

"She's not just any little girl." Ariel squirms in her seat. "She's the light of your life, the apple of your eye, and your wife's daughter. I'm terrified of stepping anywhere near those shoes, and I'm not ready to fill them. What if she doesn't like me? What if she hates me? Or worse? What if she resents me?"

"Trust me, Callie already thinks the world of you. You're a hero in her eyes."

"I'm no hero." ·

I tug at her chin and force her to look at me. "You're that and more. Few people would do what you have done. Now, come. Callie's waiting. She's an incredibly well-adjusted child, and she knows you're not trying to replace her mother."

"Ugh … I can't believe you're making me do this. Can't we just go back to my place and fool around?"

"Oh, we're going to do a whole lot more of that." I give her a wink.

I get out of the car and come around to her side. Opening the door, I hold out my hand. When she tries to pull her hand out of mine, I shake my head and tighten my grip.

"Relax."

"Easy for you to say," she quips, "but I'd feel more comfortable standing on my own."

Her feisty attitude is a major turn-on. As much as I want to turn around and spend another day in the sheets, this needs to happen.

"Your days of standing alone are over, and I want Callie to see what you mean to me. I have no intention of hiding my love or my affection for you. I don't think that's healthy."

"You're an unusual man. You know that, Aiden Cole?"

"Hm, using my full name? That makes me think I'm in trouble."

"And what if you were? We could make a jar for you …"

"While I appreciate the thought, that doesn't appeal to me." I stop her and lift her chin to face me. "I like being in charge."

She gulps.

"Now, all you need to think about is whether you like that too. Until then, we should probably go inside."

I've given her a lot to think about. Maybe too much, but I'm not ashamed of my desires. She wants to slow down that part of our relationship, which I'm fine with, but she's about to find out how incredibly patient I can be. Besides, I have a lifetime to bring her around to my way of thinking.

I lead her into the restaurant to the back left corner, to where Callie informed me she and Mary are sitting.

My beautiful daughter looks up from her scribbling and claps her hands when she sees us. The plan is for her to remain at the table and let me bring Ariel over. Instilling manners in my daughter is a never-ending battle.

To my dismay, but not surprise, Callie jumps up and races to Ariel. My daughter wraps her tiny arms around Ariel's waist and squeezes tiger-tight, as she calls it.

Ariel gives me an uncertain look, then lifts her arms, and very awkwardly places them around Callie's shoulders.

My daughter looks up with her biggest grin. "Daddy says I get to be the flower girl at the wedding. I already know the color of the dress I'm going to wear."

All color drains from Ariel's face, and I can't help but laugh. Mary slips out of the booth, comes over, and peels Callie off Ariel. She gives Ariel a quick look over, then glances at me and gives a nod of approval.

"It's nice to meet you, Ariel." Mary pulls Ariel into a hug. "Pretend you didn't just hear Callie say that. She likes to steal her daddy's thunder." Mary bends down and whispers into Callie's ear. "Now, what did we say about letting your dad ask her first before you started pestering her with questions about the color of your dress?" Mary practically drags Callie back to the booth.

Ariel turns to me and places a hand on her hip. "I'm not sure I can pretend I didn't hear that."

"Well, that's a shame, but it doesn't matter."

"Why?" Her eyes shimmer, and I hope it's with joy and not fear. This would be a bad time for Ariel to cut and run.

"Because my proposal is pretty badass. It's going to knock your socks off."

"I don't think we should be talking about proposals, weddings, and the color of your daughter's dress. She doesn't even know me, and we barely know each other. Julian was intense, and intense experiences tend to intensify emotions. What if you find out I'm boring as hell?"

I pull her into my embrace and give stink-eyes to my daughter for ruining my plans. Callie sticks her tongue out at me, teasing back.

"I could never find you boring." I tug her toward the booth.

"We just met." She runs her fingers through her hair. "I know we've been joking about it, but maybe we need to slow down, and that other thing too?"

"We're already slowing the swat jar down, but this thing between us is inevitable. I'm not willing to wait another minute. You feel what we have. You can't deny it, and you know we belong together. It's fate, and you can't ignore fate. We have an insane connection."

"But isn't that the very reason to take a step back? Reevaluate?"

"You think this is too fast?"

"I do." She nibbles at her lower lip but doesn't pull away. She feels the truth between us.

"No maybe about it. We're nuclear explosive hot. Melt the panties—"

"Um," she looks around to see who overhears. "Maybe not the best thing to say in public?" She leans to whisper in my ear. "Or where your daughter can hear."

"Why? It makes you blush, and I love the way you blush."

"Aiden … we should get to know each other better."

"And yet, you know I'm right. You're the one I want, and if you don't say yes today, I'll keep asking every day until there's a ring on your finger. And for the record, Callie's favorite color is pink. I highly suggest pink for her dress."

Ariel glances at Callie, who looks on with bright, starry eyes. Ariel turns her attention back to me. "You know what?"

"What?"

"I have a number in my head. Guess right and I'll marry you today."

"And if I guess wrong?"

"Then you'll have to ask me every day until you guess right."

"As long as I get to pick a number between one and one."

"Let's try one and a hundred." She gives a wink. "I think that's long enough to know if we'll last."

"The odds are in my favor. You're totally saying yes, but I'll play your game, with a catch."

"What's that?"

"You don't leave my side. You sleep in my bed every night, and you let me show you a taste of the things I like."

"Such as?"

"Why swatting your ass is a total turn-on for me, for starters."

"That's just a start?"

"Luv, it's only the beginning."

"Well, let's get started then." She leans forward and grips my shirt.

I'm ready to begin our life together.

She clasps my hand and grips it hard.

As I sit with my three best girls, there's no doubt about the truth of what Ariel says. I look forward to an amazing future. The best days of my life are ahead of me.

With a silent nod, I give thanks to my late wife for her wisdom, her love, and her incredible gift. Samantha wanted me to find love again. I've done much more than that.

I found my one.

Chapter Twenty-Three

Ariel

I<small>T TAKES FOUR MONTHS, BUT</small> A<small>IDEN FINALLY WRANGLES ME INTO A</small> white dress. I wear it now, praying I don't stain the fancy white satin with my nervous sweat.

Mary says I look beautiful, but I'll know the truth when Aiden sees me walking down the aisle.

Callie dances around me; her pink camouflage skirt floats around her ankles.

"Look at me," she cries. "I'm a princess, just like you Ariel!"

"Yes, you are so very pretty!" I grab Callie's hands and spin in a circle with the little girl.

"You're pretty! And you look like a princess, but not a mermaid!" Callie's enthusiasm is difficult to contain. Fortunately, Mary has much more practice than I do when it comes to bundling up all that energy into something useful.

"Callie," Mary says, "don't you think you need to check on the flowers?"

The floral arrangements arrived earlier in the day and passed both my and Mary's approval.

"I already checked on them. They're pretty."

"Can you do me the biggest favor?" Mary smiles at me and gives a slow shake of her head.

"Yes, Grans!" Callie bounces on her feet.

"Make sure they're perfect. Can you do that?"

"Oh yes!" Callie gives a little clap. "I can."

"Good." Mary guides Callie toward the door. "You go do that and come back and let us know."

Callie skips out of the room, and I breathe out a sigh, not realizing how much tension I've been holding in.

"She can be a handful," Mary says.

"Callie's wonderful. She's been so helpful."

"Ariel," Mary puts her hands on her hips, "don't do that."

"Do what?"

"It's okay to want a moment alone."

"I don't mind Callie. This is a big day for her, too."

"It's a bigger day for you." Mary gives me one of her stern expressions. "You don't have to share it with a nine-year-old."

"But …"

"But nothing. We're not playing this game. This is your day, not hers."

"Mary, I can't thank you enough …" The last thing I want is to insert a wedge between Aiden and his family. Mary and Callie are his life.

"Hun, you need to promise me something."

"Anything."

"You're marrying the most amazing man in the world. At one time, he was married to my daughter. They loved each other, and their love was tragically cut short, but that was a long time ago."

"I know."

"You know nothing."

"I don't understand."

"This is your time. Sam knew something Aiden didn't. She understood the kind of man he is, what he's capable of. You don't have to feel guilty for taking his love. You're not filling her shoes. You're not taking away from the love they shared."

"Then why does it feel that way?"

"You're taking Aiden in a completely different direction. He loves you. Own it. Accept it, and be proud of it. Samantha would want nothing less for him."

"But Callie?"

"Callie knows her mother's wishes. You're not expected to fill that role, although I already see love blossoming between you and Callie. What the two of you have will be something unique to you. Focus on that. You're not her mother, but you will be the most amazing influence in her life. Show her what it means to love and you'll honor her mother's memory."

"You're incredible, Mary. Has anyone ever said that to you?"

She smiles. "No, but I know."

I don't respond. Mary loves her late husband. She might date and play the field, but she holds onto her late husband's love. She mourns him but realizes the greatest gift he gave her, the same gift Samantha gave Aiden, was the gift of loving another.

"I didn't think I'd be this nervous." I tug on the silk of my dress, ashamed to admit my fears.

A soft knock on the door sounds.

"You ready?" Andrew's soft voice fills the silence between me and Mary.

I clear my throat. "I'm ready."

Andrew opens the door. He and Larry look comical, and yet incredibly perfect, in their pink camouflage tuxedoes. Callie's dress matches them perfectly.

"Can we come in?" Larry calls out from behind Andrew.

"Yes!" I fan my face, pushing back the tears. "Come in."

Andrew and Larry walk in, looking uncomfortable entering the bridal suite. I don't have female friends to stand by me, so I asked Andrew and Larry to fill that role as I exchange vows with Aiden.

They were honored, and then appalled, when I revealed Callie's obsession with pink camouflage.

A small ceremony, all the important people are present. There are a few on my side of the aisle. With my parents no longer with me, I nonetheless feel their ethereal presence and their love. I may not have many friends, but it's not like I'm alone.

Over the past four months, I opened up with Andrew and Larry, welcoming them into my life by sharing more of myself. They love Aiden, respect the hell out of him, and bonded over the whole hurricane thing. Andrew and Larry eagerly stand by me, bridesmen of the most unusual variety.

The entire wedding breaks all the rules.

My bridesmaids are two grown men, one married and one engaged. They initially balked at the pink wedding theme but relented when Callie showed them the pink and gray camouflage she picked out for her daddy's wedding.

I didn't know they made tuxes in pink camouflage, but Aiden's mother-in-law turned into a miracle worker.

Pink camouflage might not be the most masculine attire, but neither are two men acting as bridesmaids. They take it in stride, loving everything about the entire situation, even as it challenges their masculinity. It's a testament to Callie's ability to convince the men in her life to bend to her wishes.

Andrew and Larry will stand with her, decked out in pink, gray, and white. Andrew's wife and kids scramble over the pews on the bride's side of the aisle, excited by the festivities. Larry's new fiancée sits with them, looking nervous but excited. It'll be her turn in less than a month.

Aiden's side of the aisle is as thin as mine, but filled with love and support. His crew from the rig support him. Randall and Duncan will stand with him at the front of the church.

I know some of the other men and their families who fill the pews. People who respect their OIM and take the time from their busy schedules to see him marry the love of his life.

I accept that role. I may not be his first wife, but I'm the one he wants.

Samantha is not forgotten in the ceremony.

Aiden let it slip that lilies were her favorite flower. He doesn't know it, and won't until I walk down the aisle, but my bouquet and the flowers twined in my veil are worn in homage to his late wife.

I owe much to Samantha's wisdom. Without her, I never would've found the love of my life.

I wait in the dressing room, nervous and afraid, as most brides are, while I fuss over my hair, my dress, and the crazy veil. Beside me, the most amazing woman holds my hand. Mary has become a dear friend and interesting confidant.

I thought it would be awkward having Aiden's late wife's mother help me with wedding plans, but Mary is a trooper. Over the past four months, we've formed a unique bond.

We.

It's a unique term.

Me and Mary.

Me and Callie.

Me, Mary, and Callie.

Me and Aiden.

And, of course, all of us together.

We form a family, tied together by circumstance and fate.

And then there are the others in the mix.

Andrew and Larry forged their way into my life. They began as fellow crewmen, men who sat in the back of my helicopter and became a part of my family. Aiden's crew does the same, extending the reach of those I hold dear.

And then there is one other, perhaps the most important, although she doesn't know it.

Brie Hamilton, the yacht captain who fished Aiden and his crew out of the Gulf after a week adrift is a very special guest.

Brie and her crew saved Aiden's life and brought him to safe harbor. I owe the quiet yacht captain a debt of gratitude.

The wedding is flawless. Aiden's eyes mist over when he sees me walking down the aisle, then again when he finally sees the flowers. Everything is perfect.

After the wedding, as I dance with Aiden, I lift my glass toward Brie and notice the handsome man standing beside her.

"I thought you said Brie was coming alone." I kiss Aiden's cheek as he pulls me into a twirl.

"Who?" Aiden looks where I point.

"Brie, the captain who fished you out of the Gulf."

Aiden glances at the pretty young woman and gives a nod.

"She had a very interesting adventure after we left her. Pirates and sunken gold. I think that's her fiancé."

"Pirates? You're kidding me."

"I wish I was, but I'm not. You should get her to tell you about how she and Brent met."

Pirates and sunken treasure? Now, that sounds like an interesting tale.

"I will."

The yacht captain has her hands wrapped around a dashing man's neck. I'm definitely interested in their story.

Aiden cups my chin and tilts my face. "You know what?"

"What?"

"Mrs. Ariel Cole, you're my one, my forever, and I'm never letting you go."

I breathe out a sigh. "There was a time something like that would have sent me running for the hills …"

"And now?"

"And now?" I let the moment stretch between us, feeling the strength of our love.

"Yes?"

"Now, I'm wondering about all kinds of things."

"Such as?" He rocks his hard body against mine, showing me how eager he is to leave the festivities.

"Such as that swat jar you have in mind."

He stumbles, bringing our dance to a halt. "Don't tease me."

"I've had time to think."

"And?"

"I'm forever and always yours."

I speak the truth, cementing my promise in his arms. I belong to him, and he belongs to me. All the rest, we'll figure out together.

The future belongs solely to us.

Forever and always.

THANK YOU FOR READING SAVING ARIEL. IF YOU ENJOYED AIDEN and Ariel's story, you'll enjoy reading Saving Brie.

Grab your copy of Saving Brie today. *Click Here.*

Get swept off your feet by a treasure hunter as you hunt for sunken Spanish gold.
When everything is put on the line, will true love prevail?
Or is this the end?
Grab your copy today!

Brie doesn't believe in true love, happily ever afters, or love at first sight. When the sexy Brent Calloway hires her to captain his research vessel sparks fly, but there's one big problem.

Some things are forbidden, like sleeping with your boss.

For Brent, however, Brie might be willing to break a few rules. He pulls her to him with an attraction she can't resist.

Only this isn't an ordinary job. Billions in Spanish gold have been lost for centuries beneath the waves and Brent's on the hunt for sunken treasure.

With treachery, betrayal, and modern day pirates eager to steal the gold, there's no time for falling in love. They must fight to save themselves—or perish beneath the waves.

Dive into *Saving Brie* by master storyteller, Ellie Masters where your happily ever after is waiting.

Read a sneak peak of Saving Brie.
Turn the page.

Saving Brie

SNEAK PEAK

"WHAT THE HELL, GUS?" I SLAM MY MUG DOWN ON THE COUNTER. "What do you mean you can't captain for me? We're supposed to ship out at first light. You can't leave me high and dry like this."

My timetable doesn't allow for delays. Stopping the operation to find a suitably licensed captain can take days, if not weeks, and by then it will be too late.

It's time to take advantage of Hurricane Julian's work. Storms of that magnitude move massive amounts of sand beneath the waves as they sweep up the Gulf. It's my hope enough sand shifts to expose what a lifetime of research says will be there, but I have to get there now.

Not weeks from now.

"Like I said," Gus gives an overly dramatic sigh. "My doc says no-go. Can't ship out." Gus has already tied on four too many beers and stares back at me with bleary eyes. He thumps his chest. "My ticker needs help."

His liver needs more help at the rate Gus pounds the beer.

"But can't you postpone your appointment for a week, or two?" I flinch at the whine in my voice and clear my throat.

All I need are a couple of days to sail down to the Keys and a week to explore the wreck I know is buried there. I stand to score the find of a lifetime; nearly a billion dollars in gold bullion.

Gus's heart isn't that sick. Is it? Although, if Gus dies while on my ship, there will be hell to pay.

"Nope." Gus takes another swig. "Gotta do the stress test tomorrow, and depending on that... " Gus leans forward; his expression dour. "Doc thinks I need to go under the knife."

I curse. Luck favors the prepared, and I've spent a lifetime getting ready for this moment. Now Gus leaves me hanging because of a bad heart?

"You can't back out." I try a different angle, and hope I don't sound as desperate as I feel. At least I no longer sound whiny. Maybe I can bully Gus into reconsidering? "We have a contract and you took an advance."

"We have an understanding." Gus sucks down the last of his beer and gives a loud belch. He waves to the bartender. "Gimme another. And if it's about the advance, I'll give it back. No worries about me keeping what ain't mine."

"You gave your word." I try to keep the irritation out of my voice, but from the wide-eyed stares of those at the end of the bar, I fail miserably to do so.

A beat-up shack, the *Tipsy Pickle*, teeters on pylons driven into the basin of the marina decades ago. The place barely passes health inspection, and probably only with a healthy exchange of under-the-table cash. Paint flakes off the weathered exterior; stale beer and dried up piss create a pungent atmosphere inside. But the alcohol is cheap and the food amazingly good.

I'm surprised the *Tipsy Pickle* hasn't been bought out, stripped down to the pylons and rebuilt to attract a more up and coming crowd. Yuppies, hipsters, and Millennials love their booze as much as anyone, and they don't blink twice at overinflated prices. The *Tipsy Pickle* doesn't attract that crowd and as far as I'm concerned sits on a goldmine.

Not that one can tell from the thin and haggard crowd.

Tired men hunch on dilapidated stools and prop weary elbows

on tables worn smooth by decades of use. Half of the tables are occupied, most by individuals not interested in sharing their beer and food with others. Music crackles through tired speakers, creating enough sound to cover most conversation without drowning it out completely.

A quick glance reveals no likely candidates for my sudden captain's vacancy. These are dockworkers and deckhands. I need a licensed commercial boat captain to pilot my research rig down to the Keys.

"What the hell am I going to do? You can't leave me hanging. Don't you know anyone who can step up?"

The door bangs open, letting in a sliver of light. By habit, I look to see who enters.

Like something out of a movie, light spills around the slender form of a woman, putting all her curves on display; and what amazing curves they are. Trim and toned, the woman has amazing tits, a tiny waist, and hips a man can grab a hold of while he pounds himself into oblivion.

I can't help but gape.

Not alone in my admiration, every head in the bar swivels to fix on the apparition.

Chin lifted, the woman pauses at the doorway and scans the interior. After seeing who's inside, I think she'll run from the rough crowd, but the woman doesn't hesitate. With effortless grace, she glides across the floor; an ethereal creature, she makes a beeline for the bar.

She picks her path with care, avoiding the occupied tables, and heads to a group of empty stools a few seats down from me and Gus. When her gaze meets mine, she smiles and it's like a choir of angels lift in song. The soft cushions of her lips part and her tiny pink tongue darts out. I can't help the natural reaction of my body and adjust my perch on the stool.

What stunning lips.

Perky and raspberry red, I debate my next move as all manner of filth runs through my mind.

With a face cut right from the pages of a men's magazine, all present track her passage. Even after she sits on the stool, all eyes remain glued to her stunning figure. If any are like me, they wonder what she might look like spread out on the cover of the annual swimsuit edition, or better yet, stretched out naked in bed.

When she glances at me, blue eyes like a calm summer sea give a slow languid blink. Her wavy brown hair, cut short at the shoulders, shimmers despite the dim lighting of the bar. She gives her hair a casual flick and my heart flutters. Her eyes narrow as she peers through the dimly lit bar, staring directly at me, then a spark of recognition flares and a smile curves those cherry red lips. She slips off her stool and comes toward me.

Feeling cockier than is wise, I prepare to charm her into my bed where I can see how close my fantasy lives up to reality.

If Gus's heart issues ruin the chance of a lifetime, at least I can spend the night with this beauty wrapped around me as I listen to her breathy moans filling the sweltering night air.

But she doesn't approach me. I'm not the object of her attention at all. She stops short, coming to stand beside Gus.

"Gus!" She gives the fat bastard a hug and kisses Gus's cheek. "How have you been?"

What the hell?

"Well, aren't you a sight for sore eyes." Gus beams at the beauty. "It's been over a year, Brie. Whatcha doing in Tampa?"

"Relocating a client's yacht. Just pulled into dock."

"Is that so?" Gus's bleary eyes brighten and he sits up a little straighter.

I peer around Gus, waiting for an introduction.

The bartender brings over wine and sets it in front of the woman. Far too inquisitive, the asshole checks out her tits with open-mouthed hunger. I want to lean over the counter and smack the prick for being such a flagrant asshole. There's a thin line separating admiration and flat out disrespect, one this guy crosses by miles.

"You headed out soon?" Gus empties his beer. This time, instead of letting his belch rip, he covers his mouth, and lets the burp slip out quietly.

"Nope." She glances at me, but makes no attempt to introduce herself.

Gus, being the ass he is, doesn't make introductions. Regardless, I hold eye contact and give her a tip of my head. In a second, I'll take care of Gus's oversight. She stares at me with curiosity flickering in the depths of her baby blues, but she dismisses me to continue her conversation with Gus.

"I've got a couple of weeks off." She sips from her drink. "Although, I may have to change that. Lost my on-time bonus with the storm." She leans close and places her hand on Gus's thigh. "And guess what?"

I can't keep my eyes off her delicate fingers and wonder what it might feel like to have her hands on me. I'm starting to hate Gus.

"What darling?" Gus eats up her attention.

"You know the rig that capsized?" Her delicate voice rise in pitch.

"It's all over the news." Gus gives a vigorous shake of his head. "They said it could've been the worst spill of the century if not for the guys who capped it before it tipped."

"Well, those guys spent a week in a lifeboat and I picked them up." Excitement lights her face with a rosy glow.

"You don't say?" Gus leans back and crosses his arms. "I'm impressed. Haven't seen anything in the news about that, but I'm not surprised. You're a real angel."

"I don't know about that, and that rescue cost me my bonus." She takes another sip, peeks at me out of the corner of her eye, then focuses back on Gus. "Know of any work?"

"As a matter of fact…" Gus slaps his palm down on the bar. He turns to me. "Looks like I found you a captain."

I jerk, not expecting the conversation to head in that direction. "A chick?"

The brunette gives a slow, disappointed shake of her head. "Yeah dick-wad, this fucking *chick* is a captain. Welcome to the twenty-first century, mate."

She certainly has the mouth of a sailor. Now why does that turn me on?

"Look, I didn't mean to offend—" I hold up a hand.

"Oh, you offended pretty damn well." She gives me the back of her shoulder. Smooth and bronze from the sun, her flawless skin practically glows.

I lean toward Gus. "Look, I need a captain with experience, not a—"

"Not a *what?*" She turns back around, showing me how poorly I keep my voice down. "You don't think girls can drive boats?"

"It's not a little boat, and yeah. I don't need a chick driving a damn boat. I've got a real ship out there."

Gus giggles. It's an odd sound coming from such a large man. The laughter turns into a wheeze and evolves into a coughing fit. The brunette gives me a sideline glare as she smacks Gus on the back until he can breathe again.

"You don't look that good." She thumps him again.

The bartender brings Gus's fifth beer over, but the girl picks up the glass and sets it out of Gus's reach.

"He's done for the night." She states, completely at ease taking control and speaking for Gus.

"You took my beer, Brie." Gus gives a little whine. "Give it back."

She peers into his eyes. "How many have you had?"

"One or two?" Gus lies, but the chick isn't having it.

She looks to the bartender who holds up five fingers.

"Yeah, that's what I thought. Pour him water and keep it coming. You're drinking two glasses of water, then I'm taking you home. You still with Stella? Or did she leave your ass?"

"Still with Stella," Gus says with a grump. "She won't leave me."

"Okay, give me your keys and I'll get you home."

Gus tugs on my shirt. "Brie's your captain. If you really want to shove off in the morning, she's your man."

"Not a man, Gus." Her gaze cuts to me, full of challenge rather than the curiosity I saw before. "I'm better than a man."

Well shit.

I stepped into that wrong. Not to mention, there will be no

twisting in the sheets with this chick, not after pissing her off in what can only be called an epic failure.

But a chick? Gus can't possibly suggest this slip of a girl has the chops, let alone the credentials and commercial license to captain my ship.

Gus leans over. "Brie's an excellent captain, man. Seriously."

"I'm not operating a weekend charter, Gus. You've seen my ship."

"I have, and Brie can handle it. She's a pro at yachts larger than your little research rig. I should know. I taught her."

I step around Gus and stand behind Brie. "Is that true?"

"Depends? What's it pay?"

"Don't you want to know how big it is?"

Her eyes cut down to my crotch, then she slowly drags her gaze back up my chest.

"In my experience, it's never good to ask a man how big something is if you want the truth. They exaggerate and I'm usually left unimpressed."

I raise a brow, loving her spirit. This chick promises to be a challenge. It's been far too long since a woman excited me.

"I've never failed to impress a woman."

"That remains to be seen." She turns to Gus. "You ready to go home?"

"I s'pose. You gonna work things out with Brent?"

"Depends on whether he's able to impress me. I still haven't heard how much, how long, or how big."

Get swept off your feet by a treasure hunter as you hunt for sunken Spanish gold.
Dive into *Saving Brie* by master storyteller, Ellie Masters where your happily ever after is waiting.

You can grab Saving Brie.
Just Click HERE

Love is everywhere in this swoon-worthy, steamy contemporary romantic suspense.

Ellie Masters The EDGE

If you are interested in joining Ellie's Facebook reader group, THE EDGE, we'd love to have you.

The Edge Facebook Reader Group
elliemasters.com/TheEdge

Join Ellie's ELLZ BELLZ.
Sign up for Ellie's Newsletter.
Elliemasters.com/newslettersignup

Books by Ellie Masters

The LIGHTER SIDE

Ellie Masters is the lighter side of the Jet & Ellie Masters writing duo! You will find Contemporary Romance, Military Romance, Romantic Suspense, Billionaire Romance, and Rock Star Romance in Ellie's Works.

Sign up to Ellie's Newsletter and get a free gift. https://elliemasters.com/RescuingMelissa

YOU CAN FIND ELLIE'S BOOKS HERE:

ELLIEMASTERS.COM/BOOKS

Military Romance

Guardian Hostage Rescue

Rescuing Melissa

(Get a FREE copy when you join Ellie's Newsletter)

Rescuing Zoe

Rescuing Moira

Rescuing Eve

Rescuing Lily

Rescuing Jinx

Rescuing Freya

Rescuing Eden

The One I Want Series
(Small Town, Military Heroes)
By Jet & Ellie Masters

EACH BOOK IN THIS SERIES CAN BE READ AS A STANDALONE AND IS ABOUT A DIFFERENT COUPLE WITH AN HEA.

Saving Ariel

Saving Brie

Saving Cate

Saving Dani

Saving Jen

Saving Abby

Rockstar Romance
The Angel Fire Rock Romance Series

EACH BOOK IN THIS SERIES CAN BE READ AS A STANDALONE AND IS ABOUT A DIFFERENT COUPLE WITH AN HEA. IT IS RECOMMENDED THEY ARE READ IN ORDER.

Ashes to New (prequel)

Heart's Insanity (book 1)

Heart's Desire (book 2)

Heart's Collide (book 3)

Hearts Divided (book 4)

Hearts Entwined (book5)

Forest's FALL (book 6)

Hearts The Last Beat (book7)

Contemporary Romance

Firestorm

Billionaire Romance

Billionaire Boys Club

Hawke

Richard

Brody

Contemporary Romance

Cocky Captain

(VI KEELAND & PENELOPE WARD'S COCKY HERO WORLD)

Romantic Suspense

EACH BOOK IS A STANDALONE NOVEL.

The Starling

~AND~

Science Fiction

Ellie Masters writing as L.A. Warren

Vendel Rising: a Science Fiction Serialized Novel

About the Author

ELLIE MASTERS is a multi-genre and best-selling author, writing the stories she loves to read. Dip into the eclectic mind of Ellie Masters, spend time exploring the sensual realm where she breathes life into her characters and brings them from her mind to the page and into the heart of her readers every day.

When not writing, Ellie can be found outside, where her passion for all things outdoor reigns supreme: off-roading, riding ATVs, scuba diving, hiking, and breathing fresh air are top on her list.

Ellie's favorite way to spend an evening is curled up on a couch, laptop in place, watching a fire, drinking a good wine, and bringing forth all the characters from her mind to the page and hopefully into the hearts of her readers.

FOR MORE INFORMATION
elliemasters.com

facebook.com/elliemastersromance

twitter.com/Ellie__Masters

instagram.com/ellie_masters

bookbub.com/authors/ellie-masters

goodreads.com/Ellie_Masters

Connect with Ellie Masters

Website:
elliemasters.com
Amazon Author Page:
elliemasters.com/amazon
Facebook:
elliemasters.com/Facebook
Goodreads:
elliemasters.com/Goodreads
Instagram:
elliemasters.com/Instagram

Final Thoughts

I hope you enjoyed this book as much as I enjoyed writing it. If you enjoyed reading this story, please consider leaving a review on Amazon and Goodreads, and please let other people know. A sentence is all it takes. Friend recommendations are the strongest catalyst for readers' purchase decisions! And I'd love to be able to continue bringing the characters and stories from My-Mind-to-the-Page.

Second, call or e-mail a friend and tell them about this book. If you really want them to read it, gift it to them. If you prefer digital friends, please use the "Recommend" feature of Goodreads to spread the word.

Or visit my blog https://elliemasters.com, where you can find out more about my writing process and personal life.

Come visit The EDGE: Dark Discussions where we'll have a chance to talk about my works, their creation, and maybe what the future has in store for my writing.

Facebook Reader Group: The EDGE

Thank you so much for your support!

Love,

Ellie

Dedication

This book is dedicated to you, my reader. Thank you for spending a few hours of your time with me. I wouldn't be able to write without you to cheer me on. Your wonderful words, your support, and your willingness to join me on this journey is a gift beyond measure.

Whether this is the first book of mine you've read, or if you've been with me since the very beginning, thank you for believing in me as I bring these characters 'from my mind to the page and into your hearts.'

Love,
Ellie

Books by Jet Masters

If you enjoyed this book by Ellie Masters, the LIGHTER SIDE of the Jet & Ellie writing duo, and aren't afraid of edgier writing, you might enjoy reading BDSM themed books written by Jet, the DARKER SIDE of the Masters' Writing Team.

The DARKER SIDE
Jet Masters is the darker side of the Jet & Ellie writing duo!

Romantic Suspense
Changing Roles Series:
THIS SERIES MUST BE READ IN ORDER.
Book 1: Command Me
Book 2: Control Me
Book 3: Collar Me
Book 4: Embracing FATE

HOT READS
A STANDALONE NOVEL.
Down the Rabbit Hole

Light BDSM Romance
The Ties that Bind

EACH BOOK IN THIS SERIES CAN BE READ AS A STANDALONE AND IS
ABOUT A DIFFERENT COUPLE WITH AN HEA.

Alexa
Penny
Michelle
Ivy

HOT READS
Becoming His Series

THIS SERIES MUST BE READ IN ORDER.

Book 1: The Ballet
Book 2: Learning to Breathe
Book 3: Becoming His

Dark Captive Romance

A STANDALONE NOVEL.

She's MINE